Revenge of the Girl with the Great Personality

ALSO BY ELIZABETH EULBERG

The Lonely Hearts Club

Prom & Prejudice

Take a Bow

Revenge of the Girl with the Great Personality

ELIZABETH EULBERG

Point

Library of Congress Cataloging-in-Publication Data Available

ISBN 978-0-545-47699-7

10 9 8 7 6 5 4 3 2 1   13 14 15 16 17

Printed in the U.S.A.   23
First edition, March 2013

The text type was set in Goudy Old Style.
Book design by Elizabeth B. Parisi

For my siblings,

Eileen, Meg, and WJ,

who never let anybody put their baby sis in a corner

Attack of the Mini Beauty Queens

Applying butt glue to my sister's backside is, without question, not the first way I'd choose to spend a weekend.

However, getting up close and personal is just one of the many glamorous tasks that are involved in being on Team Mackenzie. My sister's a beauty queen, and she's owning this room. I can't help but feel a small sense of pride while watching Mac strut onstage in her (non-riding-up) bikini in front of an audience.

I do realize how pathetic this makes my life sound.

Sometimes I can't believe that Mackenzie and I are related. Even the middle-aged man next to me currently taking photos of her gave me a *yeah-right* look when I told him we were sisters. Not like I care what he thinks. *He's* the creepy one here.

Mac is one of those girls with shiny hair and gorgeous skin. You know the ones that I'm talking about.

I'm currently surrounded by them.

Even the most self-confident girl (who, to put it politely, does not possess any of the above mentioned characteristics) can feel a little down spending an entire day with the Beauty Bots.

There Mac is in the spotlight, smiling away as her (mostly fake) blond-highlighted hair bounces in the air. She twists and turns to the music blaring during the swimsuit competition. Her tanned legs (done in the hotel room bathroom last night) hit the mark as she shows off her white teeth (also fake) to the three judges in front of her. She bats her lashes (well, *some* belong to her) flirtatiously to the one male judge. Her red-sequined two-piece suit (I spent all week trying to get her to sit still for me to take it in) sparkles in the spotlight. It took two spa visits, one salon appointment, a hair and makeup stylist, one pageant coach, one seamstress sister, and one very stressed-out mother for her to arrive at this moment.

The music ends and she gives one final bow before she struts off stage.

"Wow, she's phenomenal," the guy next to me says.

I give him a look that makes it clear that I'm beyond disgusted by his interest in my sister.

Oh, did I forget to mention that Mackenzie is seven years old?

Yep. *Seven*.

I walk over to the side of the stage. Mom's suffocating Mac with a giant hug of congratulations.

"Oh, sweetie, you were incredible. I'm so proud of you!" Mom wipes the sweat off her brow. She spent Mac's entire routine behind the judges, duplicating the moves. I used to be right by her side, but now I prefer to watch from the back. It's enough that I'm wearing a GO MACKENZIE! shirt with Mac's latest glamour shot on it. While this new one doesn't have glitter all over it like the others, her two eyeballs line up at a very unfortunate place on me.

"Wasn't this the best you've seen her, Lexi?" Mom blasts me with her overexaggerated smile.

"You were great, Mac," I say, stuffing my hands in my pockets. I once gave Mac a huge hug after one of her routines and a bobby pin got caught on my sleeve. When I pulled away, half her hair went with me. I learned a very important lesson that day: Hands off the talent.

"We've got to get you back into your gown for crowning!" Mom grabs Mac's hand as we walk out of the room. Mom turns her head to me. "I've got it from here, Lexi."

I stop as I watch them get into the elevator without me.

While I should be grateful to have a few moments to myself to recover from the last several hours of constant running around, I can't help but feel like I'm being left out of some quality mother-daughter time. But today's Mackenzie's day.

I turn around and head to the hotel lobby. I sit down on an over-stuffed chair, close my eyes, and remember a different, simpler time. A time before pageants. A time before Miss Mackenzie came into our lives.

I was an only child for the first nine years of my life. I remember being little and wanting to have a baby brother or sister (or a dog), but then the fighting started. At first, my parents would hardly speak. I remember thinking something was wrong. We'd be at the kitchen table and it'd be silent. Not the good, peaceful quiet, but the unnerving kind. I'd attempt to shatter the silence barrier by telling them something I learned in school — the name of the fifth president, the capital of Wisconsin, the meaning of *onomatopoeia*. All I'd get in return was a strained "that's nice" between bites.

I started to relish the quiet once the yelling began. I would sit in my room and put my head under my pillow, pretending that I was part of one of those perfect families I'd seen on TV. Then something weird happened. Mom and Dad suddenly started to act all lovey-dovey around each other. I thought everything was going to be back to normal. Then I found out Mom was pregnant. I guess they thought having another kid would save their marriage.

Several months later, Mackenzie was born. But Dad left anyway. Mac wasn't even a year old.

So there's a nine-year age difference between Mackenzie and me. I do my best to be the caring and fun older sister. I also wanted to make up for the fact that Dad wasn't around. And selfishly, I thought having a little sister would fill the emptiness I felt in our family.

Mom found something else to fill that void.

2.

Obsession Actually

The bright spot of going to pageants nearly every weekend is also one of the most problematic: a boy. After all, most trouble usually starts with a boy. But he's not just any boy. No, he's possibly the most amazing, hottest, and sweetest boy ever known to teenage kind.

Okay, this is probably the point where I should mention that I sometimes have difficulty focusing on anything whenever Logan comes up. I'm usually a pretty together person, but whenever I'm around him, I melt into this giddy, brainless, gooey lump of my former self.

Since he's currently walking over to me, I start to focus on my breath. *Easy, tiger, you can handle this.*

"There you are!" Logan says, and I try to keep my heart from floating out of my body when he smiles at me. "You can*not* leave me alone in there. That's cruel and unusual punishment." He winks one of his deep green eyes at me.

I feel the heat rising in my cheeks . . . and elsewhere. "Yeah, especially the unusual part. I'm not sure, but did that one mom dress her newborn up as a cowgirl or a stripper?"

He sits down on the couch next to me. Like, *right* next to me. "It's hard to tell sometimes, especially when sequined leather chaps are involved."

I give a little laugh, all while reminding myself to keep my wits. I swear, one of these days I'm going to totally lose it and attack him. I'll be on the cover of magazines as The Teen Terror, and they'll make a made-for-TV movie about me where they'll have me hiding in the bushes and sending him lockets of my hair. (I hid in his bushes once, but that was on a dare from Benny.)

I'm pretty sure Logan knows I have a crush on him. I mean, how could he not? Pretty much every girl in school does. Except Cameron, who thinks he's a bit too "clean cut" and "boring" (*blasphemy!*). And *she's* supposed to be the smart one.

Logan's talking to me like it's no big deal, but I'm transfixed by every curve of his face, every piece of sandy blond hair on his head. I find my gaze shifting down toward his lips. *Oh, those lips* . . . which are in the middle of telling me some story.

Come on, Lexi. Concentrate.

I dig my fingernails into my arm.

". . . is ridiculous, don't you think?" Logan finishes his story and looks at me for some sort of reaction.

I stall for a few moments by pretending to look thoughtful.

What could he have said that agreeing with him would be the wrong answer? It's not like there was any way he would say something like, *"You know the criticism the Nazis get is ridiculous, don't you think?"*

He's clearly looking for me to agree with him. So I go for broke. "Yeah."

"Exactly." He nods appreciatively at me.

Phew.

Logan, completely oblivious to my nerves, grabs my sleeve and gives it a playful tug. "Nice shirt, by the way."

Ugh, this silly shirt. I decide to do what I do best. Go for the Miss Self-Deprecating crown.

"Thanks. I'm trying to win Most Non-Photogenic today." I gesture down at my hideously embarrassing T-shirt, rolled-up jeans, and canvas shoes. "I think there should be a special award for NO hair and makeup." My hair is in a messy ponytail and I think at some point this morning I put on lip balm. I don't see the point in trying to put any effort into my appearance on days like this, even though I know Logan's going to be here. It would be futile to try to compete under these circumstances.

"That's because you don't *need* hair and makeup." He nudges my leg with his knee. "Do you see what these girls look like when they arrive?"

I try to not read into what Logan's saying. I'd only be torturing myself thinking that he sees me as anything but a friend. Because while I'm here with my sister, he's here with the ultimate beauty queen.

Alyssa Davis.

A.k.a. future Miss Texas.

A.k.a. Logan's girlfriend.

Alyssa deserves all the accolades she gets because she's the epitome of a beauty queen: honey-colored hair with blond highlights framing her heart-shaped face. She even has these Disneyesque blue eyes that I swear actually sparkle.

It's so not fair.

"Come on." Logan gets up off the couch and extends his hand. "They'll kill us if we miss the crowning." I take his hand to stand and then he puts his arm around my shoulder. I try to steady my breath. Logan's always been very touchy-feely with me, but I still get butterflies in my stomach. *Every. Single. Time.* Of course, with me Logan just rubs my back or gives me these huge hugs that lift me up. It's always very safe, very friendly. Unfortunately.

We enter the hotel conference room and the anxiety in the room practically knocks us over. All the parents, kids, and coaches are staring up at the podium as if their lives depend on the results.

"Hey." Logan gently nudges my arm as I'm about to sit with my mom and Mac. "You going to Josh's party tonight?"

I shake my head. I didn't even know that Josh was having a party. But I like Logan even more for thinking that we run in the same circles.

Luckily, I don't have to bring him down to reality since I have a good excuse. "Can't," I tell him. "I have to work."

"Too bad." Logan seems genuinely sad. "Well . . . I guess I'll see ya later." He gives me another wink before he walks over to Alyssa.

So, when he said "too bad," do we think he meant "too bad that you have to be stuck on a Saturday night in the prime of your youth to work at the mall" or "too bad because I was going to dump Alyssa and make out with you all night"?

See what I did there?

If I don't watch it, I'll let one tiny comment from Logan send me off into the delusional deep end. I know it's ridiculous, but I can't help it. It doesn't really matter what he *says*. The fact is, he has a girlfriend.

All I need to do is look over and see his arms wrapped around Alyssa's tiny waist as he gazes happily into her eyes, and I come tumbling back to reality.

3.

The Good, the Bad, and the Great Personality

I used to think that I could someday have a shot with Logan. Like if Alyssa got carted off to someplace that didn't have phone or Internet access . . . and you couldn't get there by any known means of transportation. Everybody can have a dream. But then I overheard Logan talking to Grant Christensen in the hallway at school before Homecoming this year. When I heard Logan say my name, I hid behind a pillar to listen in on his conversation. As one does.

"Why don't you ask Lexi?" Logan said.

"Lexi Anderson?" I couldn't see what Grant's face looked like, but from the sound of his voice, he didn't seem pleased by Logan's suggestion.

"Yeah, she's the best." My heart flew up into my throat. "She's super funny and has such a great personality."

And there it was.

GREAT PERSONALITY.

It wasn't the first time I'd heard this phrase. It wasn't even the worst circumstance in which it had been used. But that didn't make it sting any less.

Oh, I'm aware it's a compliment. Really. Much better than having a bad personality or, in the case of some girls at my school, no personality at all. But still. When a guy uses *great personality* to describe a girl, it's the polite way of saying *fat and ugly.*

Okay, maybe that's a little harsh, but Logan was basically saying, *"Lexi is great to hang out with, someone who can keep a conversation going, but she isn't someone you'd want to date. She's not one of* those *girls."*

In other words, I'm the girl that all the guys go to because, well, I'm the cool chick who they can talk to about the girl they *really* like. Especially when their perfect girlfriend is busy changing into another pageant outfit.

I guess I'm not fat. I don't need a forklift to leave the house (although Mom isn't far behind from that milestone; she now needs two seats to fly). One of the benefits of having a morbidly obese mother is that it has made me overly paranoid about my weight. I stick to mostly non-processed foods, which is basically the opposite of what Mom eats.

So I'm not fat and I'm not the most disgusting girl in my class, but I'm nowhere near the prettiest. I'm average.

I have brown hair and brown eyes. I'm not tall, I'm not short. I'm average.

And being average is fine and all, especially when you have such a *great personality*, but it means that I have zero success as far as boys go.

Are you ready for the most pathetic, woe-is-me story you've ever heard? I'm sixteen and I've never been on a date. I've never had a real kiss. (Getting chased around a table in kindergarten and kissed by Neil Blount doesn't count.) I try not to think about it, because it isn't that big of a deal. But sometimes I can't help but fear that my life will one day become legend at LBJ High. *"Did you hear about that junior who never had a boy ask her to do anything? She died alone, surrounded by her forty-two cats. Her ghost haunts the AV closet in hopes that a nerd will accidentally brush against her while getting a projector."*

I know I shouldn't care and that boys are stupid, girl power, etc. But I want, just once, for a guy to like me. Or to at least notice me. I spend so much time at these silly beauty pageants, it's hard for me to look in the mirror and not feel inadequate. Sure the pageants *allegedly* build self-esteem for the contestants, but they make me feel like a freak because *I'm* the different one there.

And believe me, I don't want to be anything like those pageant girls. But it would be nice to be asked out. Or to have someone have a crush on me for a change.

What's worse is that I hate that this makes me turn into a self-loathing, needy girl because I don't have the attention of one guy. Or, if I'm being honest, any of them.

I know that once I leave high school and go to college, it'll be different. There's got to be someone out there who's willing to give a girl with a great personality a shot.

But for now, I have to bide my time and wait for the moment when the Great Girls inherit the earth.

4.

An Ego Grows in Texas

Mackenzie is crowned a Princess in her age division. She receives a small crown and a white sash with *Princess* printed in pale pink cursive. Mac's beaming like she's won the whole pageant, but pretty much every girl who doesn't win a category like talent or beauty, or get an overall title (where you receive money), gets the Princess title. There are four other Princesses in her age group, but neither Mom nor Mac seems to notice or care. We've got yet another crown to add to her overflowing mantel.

Even though she didn't place or earn any of our entry money back, a crown's enough for her and Mom. Her name got called and she got to go on stage and get her picture taken with Alyssa, the Ultimate Grand

Supreme winner. This small victory will give Mac and Mom the motivation to get ready for the next pageant. And from our little Dallas suburb, there's one that's within driving distance practically every weekend.

The whole pageant thing started innocently enough. I guess most addictions do. Shortly after Dad left, we were at the mall and there was a modeling contest for ages sixteen and younger. I refused to take part, since I was in my rebellious-child-of-divorce stage at the time, which isn't something I've entirely grown out of. So Mom decided to sign Mac up, and she won her age group. Never mind that she was the only kid under the age of two to enter. Mom loved the attention, the validation she got that her child was the best at something. Another one of the mothers suggested pageants to her, and Team Mackenzie has been doing them ever since.

At first I happily went along, to cheer on my baby sis. But soon I started to feel like the third wheel. The older I got, the more I realized how much these pageants objectify young girls, and how much the price of the pageant was more than we could handle financially *and* emotionally. But there was no way to protest. Nothing else made my mother happy. We're a pageant family.

Sometimes I do get sad, though. Not because Mac doesn't win, but that we spend all this time and money (that we do not have) to come home with nothing more than a cheap plastic crown. The one she got today is already broken.

"Mama!" Mac screams from the backseat of the car. "Fix it!"

"Honey, I can't, I'm driving." Mom glances in the rearview mirror and starts to sweat. I'm sure she's not happy that their prized possession hasn't even survived the car ride home.

"PULL OVER!" Mac screams.

I look at my watch and it seems that Mac's normal post-pageant breakdown is right on time. I can't really blame her for being crabby; we've been up since five this morning getting ready. She's had people poking at her all day with makeup wands and curling irons, plus Mom feels the need to remind her umpteen times to smile on stage. Sometimes I want to throw a fit, but alas, someone needs to be the calm one in the family.

"Sweetie, I can't pull over," Mom calls out to an increasingly agitated Mackenzie. "We're on a tight schedule. Lexi has to get to work. Give your crown to her and she can fix it."

Mac reluctantly hands me her crown.

"Lexi, fix it," Mom orders, fatigue from the day showing in her face. "Just do this one thing for your sister."

This one thing? I resist the urge to remind Mom that I gave up my entire weekend to drive with them to Livingston. That I spend hours each week sewing Mac a new costume or driving her to dance lessons. That I have to do insane, completely abnormal things like apply *butt glue* to my sister.

But it's been a long day for us all, so I keep quiet and examine the crown. The tiny side comb used to hold the crown to the head has snapped off. "Can you please hand me my sewing kit?" I ask Mac.

She fishes for my kit in the back of the car, which is jammed with crates and hanging bags filled with all her pageant gear. She gives a little *humph* when she finally hands it over to me. I take fabric glue and apply it to the crown, willing it to hold so we don't have to listen to a tantrum for the remaining three hours.

While Mac's being grouchy now, she usually thanks me the next day when she's been able to get her beauty sleep. I know she's appreciative to have me there as a sane person to go to when Mom goes into one of her Pageant Panics. (One time, Mom suggested that Mac have mascara tattooed on her to save time each pageant — I wish I were joking.)

I turn my attention toward the broken tiara. As I hold the comb in place, I notice that the sequins are starting to fall off. "This thing is beyond cheap," I say. Then I can't help asking, "How much money did we spend this weekend?"

"None of your business," Mom says coldly.

It kind of *is* my business. I don't have a job for pocket change. I have a job so I can eat. Dad's child support goes mostly to the rent while every, and I mean *every*, cent Mom makes at the SuperStore goes to the pageants. So if I want to go out with friends or eat organic fruits and veggies instead of fast-food crap for every meal, I need to pay for it. Not to mention the fact that I want to spend the summer in New York City to attend the Fashion Institute of Technology's summer program. All of that, everything, needs to come from my money. The only time the pageant money was used for me was when I wanted to take sewing lessons. And I was only given that so I could become Mackenzie's Official Seamstress.

"Give it back!" Mac starts kicking my seat. "I want my crown."

"I need the glue to dry."

Mac screams, "I want it back NOW!"

I turn around. "Just give me a few more minutes, *please*. Believe me, I do not want your crown."

"Lexi!" Mom raises her voice at me. "Give your sister back her crown."

Seriously? Why am I the bad guy in this situation? I gently hand Mac her crown back. "Be careful, the glue hasn't dried yet."

I hear Mac whisper something that sounds like "thank you."

"Honestly, Lexi . . ." Mom doesn't finish the sentence. It just hangs in the air. And then she has to go and finish it. "You shouldn't be jealous of your sister."

Knots begin forming in my back from tensing up. "Why would I be jealous of her?"

Mom sighs. "You know . . ."

"No. I don't." Even though I do. But I'm really in no mood for it right now. I still have to work the closing shift. While they get to spend the evening at home watching TV, I have to be on my feet until almost midnight.

"Oh, Lexi, I know it's hard for you to have your baby sister get all the attention."

I'm not envious of Mackenzie because of the pageants. I *pity* her. That's why I don't usually get annoyed when she has one of her temper tantrums. She really doesn't know better.

I try to keep my voice level as I say, "No, it's not."

Mac's voice comes from the backseat. "You're just jealous because you're ugly."

And like that, the camel's back has been broken. I turn around and see panic flicker in her eyes. She knows she's gone too far. But instead of forgiving her, I say, "Yeah, well, I'd rather be ugly on the outside than on the inside. I can be painted up to look like one of your precious beauty queens, but you're always going to be an ungrateful brat."

I instantly regret it.

"LEXI!" Mom nearly runs off the side of the road as she smacks me on the leg.

I know I went too far. I know what I said was rude. I know I should apologize.

But calling me ugly is not okay.

I do my best to zone out Mom as she starts lecturing me about being a good sister and not egging Mac on. There's no point in arguing. Mom will never take my side on anything.

It's Mackenzie's World. I just live in it.

5.

The Semester of Our Discontent

I really wish someone had given me a heads-up that it was Popular People Night at the mall.

"Um, I don't know." Brooke holds up a size-two denim miniskirt to show Hannah. "Look how huge this is. It'll *never* fit me." The skirt is the size of a washcloth. However, Brooke's right, it probably would fall off her bony frame. "Can you see if you have a size zero?" she says loudly, ensuring everybody in the store can hear her.

I smile politely and head back to our storage room. I don't usually feel this uncomfortable when I have to wait on people from school, but Brooke likes to bark orders at me. I try not to take it personally; she's always ordering someone around, and at least *I'm* getting paid. I find her non-size size and take a deep cleansing breath before going back out onto the Brooke battlefield.

"Oh, you found it," she says dismissively as she grabs the skirt out of my hand.

Oh no, it's not customary to thank a person for doing something for you. It is I who should be thanking you, dear Brooke, for allowing me to wait on you.

Of course I keep my mouth shut. There are certain scenarios (pageants) and people (the Popular Posse) that require me to keep my thoughts in my head. I didn't say anything when Brooke started a "Katie Francis is a Skank" page after Katie beat Brooke for cheer captain. Or when Brooke started the rumor that Cam cheated on her physics final since Cam wasn't just one of the few who passed, but she aced the test.

The last thing I want is to become another victim of Brooke's wrath.

To be fair, not all of the Popular Posse are as obnoxious as Brooke. Hannah's pretty nice. And as much as that pains me since she's with Logan, so is Alyssa. Meanwhile, the guys are just guys. Unless you're a football or a walking version of a Victoria's Secret catalog, they don't really seem to care.

Brooke comes out of the dressing room wearing the skirt and a tight tank top, leaving little to the imagination. She flips her shiny black hair (she's always flipping it, or putting it up in a ponytail, or doing something to draw attention to the fact she has hair that defies the Texas heat) and studies herself in the mirror. "I think this is perfect for Josh's party," she says.

I turn my attention to a row of T-shirts that need to be refolded, but all I can hear is Brooke's loud voice echoing in our now nearly empty store.

"Josh has the best parties. *Everybody* is going to be there."

I hear Hannah murmur in a low voice, probably trying to attempt some sort of friendly wisdom on Brooke.

"Hey, Lexi!" Brooke calls sweetly to me. "I think I'm all set. Do you mind ringing us up?"

I give her a smile as I take her handkerchief — I mean *skirt* — to the register. I remind myself about what Cam once told me about Brooke. They used to be friends eons ago (grade school) and Cam said that Brooke is one of the most insecure people she's ever known, which is why she overcompensates by being loud. So maybe she isn't as bad as she sometimes puts on.

"Oh my God, look at this!" Brooke picks up a pair of pants from the plus-size display. "Oink! Oink!" She steals a look at me. "No offense."

Or not.

I don't want to be shallow, although that's laughable when in the presence of Brooke. But I think I have a way better body than her. I know that sounds conceited, but at least I have some muscle and fat. I have something that could be considered a figure, while Brooke is a walking skeleton with a ginormous push-up bra. I can't understand why guys fall for it.

But they do.

*   *   *

23

I meet Benny and Cam for my half-hour break at the food court (a.k.a. The Court).

"You'll split fries with me, won't you?" Cam greets me as I sit down at their table.

Benny gives me a smile, then motions at Cam. "The girl's craving fries and I've given up carbs."

I bite my tongue so I won't say "again." Benny's always on some sort of diet. It never lasts long. He's just a big teddy bear, and I honestly couldn't imagine him any other way. But of course I don't say any of this because Benny abhors his nickname since middle school, Benny the Bear. As much as we try to tell him it's because his last name is Bayer, we all know the truth.

I shake my head. "I can't. I already had some today."

Cam's mouth is agape. "You ate fries without me? This friendship is so over." She gets up and heads over to the burger place.

I pull out my protein bar and start to nibble on it.

Benny picks at his salad. "So how did our precious baby girl do today?"

"I handled myself well, thank you very much."

He chuckles. "Good to know, since I was obviously talking about you."

"I can't imagine you'd be referring to anybody else."

Cam puts her tray of greasy yet delicious-smelling fries down. Both Benny and I eye it with envy. "Today must've been bad if *you* ate fries," Cam observes.

"We were running late and Mackenzie got to pick the drive-thru for dinner, so . . ."

Benny leans in. "And which fine establishment did our young princess pick?"

"McDonald's."

He nods approvingly. "Ah yes, nice crisp french fry, perfect salt-to-potato ratio. Well played, Mackenzie. Well played."

I can't help but notice that Benny's eyes have been darting at something behind me ever since I sat down.

"What are you looking at?" I begin to turn around, but Benny grabs my hand.

"Don't!" he hisses.

"Um, okay." I give him a weird look while Cam blatantly turns her head to stare.

"Are you looking at —"

Cam's interrupted as a nearly empty bottle of soda flies from the opposite direction, smacking Benny in the head.

"Ouch!" His hand flies up to the place on his head where the bottle made contact.

Cam and I look behind Benny to see these kids (make that jerks) who are probably twelve or so laughing a few tables away. I'm not sure, but I think I hear one of them say "freak."

Cam gets up and strides over to the table. "Listen here, you losers, you better go over there and apologize to my friend." Cam's petite, but not someone you want to mess with.

The three boys continue to laugh. One of them, in a baseball hat and baggy jeans that fall below his butt (it's like he picked out his outfit in the Future Thugs "R" Us catalog), stands up and faces Cam. My pulse begins to quicken. "Yeah, who's gonna make me? Your little *girlfriend?*"

Cam grabs the boy by his collar and brings him so they're face-to-face across the table. I feel Benny's hand wrap tightly around my arm.

"How about your mother, Thomas. How does *that* sound?"

The kid looks like he's seen a ghost. Cam lets go of him and reaches in her pocket for her cell phone. She begins to dial, but the kids start to disperse.

"Sorry! Sorry!" they mumble as they run past us.

Both Benny and I are speechless as Cam returns to our table. She sits down and starts eating her fries like nothing happened.

I finally find my voice. "That . . . was . . . *awesome.*"

Cam smiles at me. "I used to babysit that kid — he was always trouble. Twenty bucks he's in juvie by his freshman year."

I turn my focus to Benny, who's staring down at the table. "Are you okay?" I ask.

"Whatever," he says softly. His face is the deepest shade of red and he refuses to look up.

I study Benny's face. He's trying to brush it off, but deep down I know it hurts him. Benny's been teased the entire time I've know him. He was taunted for being big when we were in grade school, but we were always close friends. He's sincerely one of the nicest people I know. But he can stand out in a crowd. Not just because of his size, but he's always worn really colorful clothing, which I like since it's better than the black and gray athletic T-shirts that fill the hallway at school. But it sort of forces you to take notice of him. I've always admired his confidence to wear what he wants. Today it's an orange *Fraggle Rock* T-shirt with matching orange All Stars.

Benny's always been Benny to me. I never thought he was different than the other guys in my class. I didn't think anything of it when he liked the same boy bands as me; I just thought he had *excellent* taste in music. By the time we were freshmen, he came out to me.

He's not "officially" out since his parents go to an extremely conservative (bordering on evangelical) church, the kind with the big-screen TVs and minister who has his own television show on, like, GOD-TV. But when Benny's with us, he can be himself. He doesn't have to worry about hiding his true colors.

It seems like we all need our safe havens to be ourselves.

"At least there wasn't much of an audience." I try to comfort Benny as I gesture at the virtually empty food court. "I think everybody's at Josh's party."

Cam raises her eyebrow at me. "How did you find out about Josh's party?"

Of course Cam knew about Josh's party. She could so run in that circle if she wanted, but she has no interest in putting up with any of their drama, and from the hallway gossip there's always something brewing with Population Popular. Plus, Cam's the smartest person in our class (if not the entire school). She's already taking AP-level classes; she might even graduate early. I sometimes feel like Benny and I bring her down, but it's her choice to be with us common folk.

We're like the Three Musketeers — all for one and all that loyalty stuff. Although we more resemble Russian nesting dolls in person — you know, the kind of dolls that stack inside of each other. On one end you have Benny the Bear, tall, big, with dark black hair that's in a shag that he sometimes tucks behind his ear when he's nervous. Then on the other end you have petite, blond Cam. Of course, I'm in the middle. Average.

Three people who look so different when they're lined up, but who just fit together. One inseparable group . . . whose separate pieces don't quite fit anywhere else.

I reach out for Benny's hand. "Are you sure you're okay?"

He pulls away from me. "It's fine."

My cheeks become flush thinking about what Benny has to put up with for just being himself. What gives anybody the right to treat someone like that?

"No. It's *not* fine, Benny. It's not." I get even more upset when I see him shrug his shoulders, like he's given up.

Benny sighs. "Lexi, let's face facts: I'm fat and gay and live in the heart of football-loving Texas. Me finding love or respect ain't gonna happen in this high school life. There really isn't anything I can do about it now, so I do my best to ignore it." His eyes once again dart quickly behind me before looking away.

I cautiously turn around and see two guys from our school chatting a few tables away.

"Benny, don't worry about those guys. I'm sure they didn't see anything," I lie. I'm pretty sure everybody saw what happened. If they didn't see the bottle hit Benny, they sure heard Cam.

"Benny?" Cam says softly. "Do you know those guys?"

He shakes his head softly. "Not really . . ."

I go to turn back around to get a better look, but Benny kicks me under the table. "Stop it! He'll see."

"Who'll see?"

Then something hits me: *Oh my God, does Benny have a crush?* I can't even hide my excitement. Benny's never had a crush on a real boy, just celebrities. So if he does, this is *huge*.

"Chris." He says it so quietly I'm not even sure that's what he's said.

I lean in so we're only inches apart. "Which one is Chris?"

"The one with the hat."

Both Cam and I try our best to nonchalantly look over at the table. Cam has it easier since she only has to look to the side. I have to basically turn all the way around. I decide to first rub my chin on my shoulder, then steal a quick glance. The guy with the hat, Chris, looks familiar. He's got a wool hat on, but has dark straight bangs swept over to the side, peeking out. He's got on a black hooded sweatshirt and black skinny jeans, with a chain that hooks his wallet to his belt buckle.

"He goes to LBJ?" Cam asks.

Benny nods. "He's in my study hall. A sophomore."

"He's cute," I offer, to see how Benny will react.

"Yeah, but he saw *everything*."

"Go talk to him!" I urge.

"Yeah!" Cam agrees. "Seize the day!"

Benny leans back in his seat. "I've been humiliated enough for one day, thank you very much."

"Benny . . ." I say softly.

"Can we please talk about something else? I can't deal with this right now. I'm sure there's some horrific story from today's pageant, right?" He looks at me expectantly.

"Well . . ." I don't want Benny to give up so easily, but I know when to not push him any further. "I think I should prepare my speech for the Worst Sister of the Year Award."

Benny's eyes get wide. "What happened?"

"Mac called me ugly."

"She did WHAT?" Cam's voice raises, and a couple near us pick up their trays and leave, probably concerned about what that girl who just scared off three boys will do next.

"Yeah, Mac called me ugly. But you know, it was at the end of the day. She was tired."

"You've got to stop making excuses for her."

"Yeah, well, she's *seven*." My mind flashes to just an hour ago. "What excuse does Brooke have?" I fill them in on what happened at work.

"Oh, Lexi . . ." Cam shakes her head. "Brooke's pure evil, and you shouldn't pay any attention to her. But as far as Mackenzie's concerned, there's absolutely no context in which it's okay to call anybody ugly."

I want to say, *And there's no context in which it's okay to throw some-thing at a complete stranger's head.* But I know Benny doesn't want to talk about it anymore.

"So what did you say?" Benny asks.

I feel even worse having to repeat those words. "I basically said that I'd rather be ugly on the outside than on the inside, and the only thing that separates me from her precious beauty queens is some makeup."

Benny looks thoughtful for a second. "You know that you're right."

"I do. I'm a horrible sister."

He shakes his head. "No. If you put some more effort into your appearance, you could look just like one of the Glamour Girls."

I laugh. "Oh, come on, there's more difference than that."

Benny sits up a little straighter. "Well, yeah. Unlike Brooke, you have an IQ *and a soul.* But the outside . . . Brooke could never be you no matter how hard she tried, but you could easily transform into one of those girls."

It would take a lot more than some foundation and lipstick to make me look like one of the Beautiful People. But I can't help smile at what Benny's said. He always knows what to do to make me feel better. Why can't he believe these kinds of things about himself?

"It's weird," I say. "Logan" — both Cam and Benny groan at the mention of his name — "basically said the same thing today. Not like anything I could do could stop him from thinking that I'm just a girl with a great personality."

"Great?" Benny teases. "I wouldn't go that far. *Adequate* perhaps."

I reach over and throw one of Cam's fries at him.

"Not the carbs!" he shouts in mock horror.

I'm happy to see a smile return to his face, especially since I have to go back to work.

As I get up to leave, I whisper into Benny's ears the three little words that make everything better, "New York City."

Benny and I have already decided that we're both going to New York once we graduate. I want to go to college at FIT and he wants to get into the creative writing program at NYU. Every once in a while, we'll go online to look at apartments and start to imagine our new lives, even if all the apartments are basically glorified closets. But that doesn't matter. All that matters is that we'll both be able to have a fresh start.

But even as I leave them, I know that's not good enough. Yes, New York will be amazing. But does Benny really need to wait another eighteen months to finally feel like himself?

I've got to figure out something to make him realize that all is not, in fact, lost.

6.

Benny and the 'Rents

*M*y mind has been swirling with what to do about Benny. It's all I could really think about this morning and afternoon. I head over to his house after work to try to encourage him to do something about Chris, even if it's a simple "hello." I hate seeing him so miserable. He deserves to have whatever or whoever he wants.

Benny's mom answers the door and gives me a big hug.

"Hi, Mrs. Bayer." I hand her a package. "This was at the front door."

She looks at the package and shakes her head. "More of those crazy T-shirts for Benjamin."

I'm always a little in awe when I walk into Benny's new, huge house. They moved in last year after his dad became a partner at his law firm.

You walk into a vast entranceway with a spiral staircase stretching up to the second floor. You could fit my entire house in the foyer. (I didn't even know what a foyer was until I saw this house and Mrs. Bayer explained.)

"How's your mom?" Mrs. Bayer asks. "We've really missed y'all in church. We'd love to have you back."

I give her a noncommittal smile. We used to go to the same massive church with Benny's family back when my family was unbroken. Many of the parishioners were really helpful to us after Dad left, providing day care and casseroles in the beginning. Then Mom got into an argument with the pastor's wife over pageants. Mom wanted some monetary help from the parish, but they didn't approve of something that valued looks over someone's faith.

There are many things that I don't agree with the church on. However, in this instance, the pastor's wife was truly preaching to the choir as far as I was concerned.

But Mom didn't see it that way. She turned her back on them and hasn't returned since.

"Well" — Mrs. Bayer can tell she's not converting me today — "anytime you need some guidance, hon."

Thankfully, Benny comes to my rescue as he descends the massive staircase. "We're doing homework. Can we meet in my room?"

"You know the rules. No girls in your room."

I was always allowed in Benny's room when I was little. But I swear, as soon as we turned twelve, Benny's parents started all these rules

34

about where we could or could not hang out together. Things got even stricter when Cam came along freshman year. Benny decided having a girlfriend would make his life easier with his family. So Cam became Benny's fake girlfriend for a couple months.

At first I was offended he didn't ask me (I can't even get a *fake* boyfriend), but as he explained, he's known me "since the womb," so Cam would be easier to explain to his parents. Now when Cam comes over, we have to stay in the living room. Even though they "broke things off amicably." It was kind of fun when it was going on, because I felt like we were playing different roles: Benny, the stud with the hot new girl in class as his girlfriend; Cam, the aforementioned girl; and me, as um, I guess the friend . . . with the great personality. *Gag*.

One perk to being seen as relatively asexual by Benny's parents is that I'm allowed in the game room, which is in an adjacent wing and has way more privacy than the living room, where the sound travels upstairs. Plus, it might possibly be the greatest room in the history of modern architecture.

Their game room has overstuffed chairs that you literally sink into and never want to leave. Plus, it has foosball *and* air hockey tables, a full-size Ms. Pac-Man arcade game (I'm currently the highest scorer, thank you very much), and pretty much every movie ever made, which we can watch on their gigantic drops-down-from-the-ceiling screen.

When I first saw this room, I immediately thought about all the amazing parties we'd have here. Then I had to remind myself that

Benny and I aren't the type of people to have parties (that people would show up for).

"Do you want to see what I got?" Benny tears open the box and pulls out a few more T-shirts. He starts excitedly showing them off to me, but I have no idea what any of them really mean.

"Who is Charles and why do you want him 'in charge' of you?" I ask.

"Are you kidding me?" Benny teases me by hanging his head in shame.

"Ah, you know I wasn't *alive* in the eighties, so . . ."

"It's called the Internet," he counters. "I found this awesome website with all these hysterical T-shirts. I bought pretty much anything that made my mom laugh or my dad groan."

"Like, totally awesome."

"*Now* you're speaking my language." Benny examines his recent purchases and I can't help but be excited for him. Sure they're just some funny shirts, but I know what it's like to have something that makes you happy. I hope to someday make clothing that makes people feel good about themselves, no matter what their size.

He gasps. "I totally forgot about this one, and I *know* you're going to approve." He holds up a T-shirt with a drawing of Beaker from *The Muppet Show*.

"You know he's my favorite!" I exclaim. I can't help but have an affinity toward Dr. Honeydew's long-suffering lab assistant. We have a lot in common: We're both forced to do degrading things at the hands of our bosses (in my case, my mother at the pageants), and we're not allowed to speak our minds. (At least I can talk, but I'm pretty sure when I do protest, my mom only hears "meep.")

"If you're lucky, I might even let you borrow it . . . as a tent." He doesn't even give me an opportunity to protest. "By the way, Mom's really excited that you're staying for dinner," he says as he packs up his purchases.

"Me too."

I went through a phase last year where I didn't like going over to Benny's house. Not because of anything the Bayers did; his parents are pretty much perfect. Well, maybe not perfect. Benny's convinced they would disown him if he told them he was gay. The pastor at his church once even referred to being gay as a "disease." But I'm not sure that's how Benny's parents would react. I see the way they look at him, and it's obvious they love him. Sometimes I think his mom knows. Or maybe I'm just transferring my ideals of a mother onto his mom.

The reason I didn't like being at Benny's house was that being with them made me realize how much my own family had deteriorated. At Benny's, everybody sits together at the table to have dinner; TV isn't allowed since it's time to catch up on everybody's day. His mom makes real food like baked chicken with rice and green beans, lasagna with salad, or (tonight's menu) roasted salmon with spinach and butternut squash.

Sitting with them makes me happy. It makes me feel like I belong somewhere.

But then I'm reminded of what I lost. What I'll never get back again.

Cam may have been Benny's fake girlfriend. But Benny's family is my fake family.

I guess in some instances, fake is better than the real thing.

"So what's the plan?" Benny brings me back to what's supposed to be our homework time.

"You mean besides me kicking your butt in Ms. Pac-Man?" I give him a mischievous grin.

"Yes, *besides* that." Benny picks up his stack of books in front of him. "Should we start with English or history?"

"I was hoping we could first talk a little bit about last night," I say cautiously.

Benny nods like he's expecting this. "Yeah, I want to talk to you about that, too."

I feel a swell of relief, hoping that Benny realizes that he's way too hard on himself.

I'm surprised when he speaks first. "Yeah, you know I love you, Lex, but you've got to stop being such a self-fulfilling prophecy."

Wait, what? He thinks that *I'm* the one with the self-esteem problem?

"Look at you. Look at what you're wearing."

"What?" I look down at my dark jeans and black V-neck top. "What's wrong with this?" It's pretty basic, but I didn't realize I was supposed to dress up for dinner at the Bayer house.

"It's only about two sizes too big. Come here." He leads me to a mirror in the hallway. He stands behind me and grabs the sides of my shirt and tightens it. "Oh, look what we have here. A figure. Curves. Aren't you the one who's supposed to be into fashion?"

I'm used to people looking at me and thinking, *You want to be in fashion?* I do love clothes, although Benny's right, I pretty much only wear jeans and cute, somewhat baggy shirts. I'll admit to being envious when I see the Glamour Girls with their expensive outfits. They usually have on the latest dresses and skirts. I don't really need to remind him why I don't bother dressing to impress.

I wiggle away from Benny. "You know why . . ." I let the words hang in the air. Benny's well aware that there was a time when I liked wearing pretty dresses and would even sneak into my mom's dresser to put on some lipstick. But we both know that girl went away a long time ago.

"But you could change all of that. You could be that girl any guy would fall for, but you don't believe in yourself. You hide behind messy hair and no makeup."

"I don't hide." For the first time possibly ever, I find myself annoyed at Benny. "And what about you?" I give him a taste of his own medicine. "It was devastating to see you yesterday. You just think you don't deserve happiness until we get to New York, but that's ridiculous, Benny. You're amazing. When are you going to see that?"

"When are you going to stop thinking that there can only be one beautiful sister in your family?" he counters.

"Well . . ." My mind races. "When are you going to put yourself out there?"

"You first."

We're both staring at each other, neither daring to blink first. Benny's lips start to quiver and I can tell he's about to crack. I hold my gaze a few more seconds before he bursts into laughter.

"I'm sorry." He holds up his hands. "I'm only looking out for you."

"Me too." And I don't know why, but I feel like humoring him. "What do you want me to do?"

His face lights up. "Wow. So many choices. Rob a bank? No, too complicated. Shave your head? No, too dramatic. How about you go up to a guy tomorrow at school and just talk to him? That's easy enough, although you can't be self-deprecating or be funny. Be you."

"But I'm *hilarious*."

He groans. "You know what I mean."

Even though I feel sick to my stomach, I find my head nodding in agreement. "Okay, but if I do this, then you need to do something for me." I reach my hand out to him. "Deal?"

He takes a moment before he hesitantly shakes it. "Deal."

7.

The Best Laid Plans of the Bitter and Fed Up

I can't believe I'm going to do this. It's not like I haven't talked to guys before, but I'm used to being the jokester. I can't believe Benny expects me to flirt with Grant "you want me to take *Lexi* to Homecoming?" Christensen.

"I heard that Grant's throwing a huge party while his parents are out of town next weekend," Benny whispers in my ear as we study Grant and Josh at their lockers. "He was bragging about it in class today and invited the usual suspects. So maybe you'll get invited!"

He's trying to sound optimistic, but I can see in his eyes that we both know this is going to end in disaster. It's not like I'm uncomfortable with making a fool of myself — I do it all the time. But being self-deprecating means that you're the one poking fun at yourself. It's others laughing *at* me that's the problem.

But if I'm going to get Benny to talk to Chris, I need to just suck it up and talk to Grant.

"Okay, I'm going to show you that this is so simple." I'm sure the quiver in my voice betrays the confidence I'm trying to project to Benny.

I decide to stop avoiding the inevitable. I can feel my heart thumping in my chest as I approach them. I don't really like Grant, but I figure it's way better to do this with someone I'm not attracted to, who doesn't already have a girlfriend.

"Hey, guys, what's up?" I lean against the locker next to Grant and pretend like it's the most normal thing in the world for me to be hanging out with him and Josh between classes.

"Ah, what's up, Lexi?" Grant gives me a little nod and waits for it. "It" is what I usually say — something funny or witty about class or a teacher. But there is nothing remotely funny about what I'm about to do. Actually, it's pretty hysterical, emphasis on the hysterical.

"Not much," I say in a hushed tone. I arch my back so my chest sticks out. I smile warmly at them both. "Just so over classes already. Can't believe we've got so much homework to do." I wrap my finger around an errant strand of hair. Maybe I should bat my eyelashes at him.

Grant nods. "Yeah, did you finish the assign —" He stops and looks at me. "Do you have something in your eye?"

Apparently my attempt at flirting resembles someone who has something in her eye. *Sexy.*

"Sorry." I smile at him, lean in, and touch him on the arm. "What were you saying?" I try to talk in a sexy low voice, but instead it sounds like I have emphysema.

I'm not exactly sure what the look is Grant is giving me, but I wouldn't be surprised if it was along the lines of *you belong in an insane asylum.* "Did you finish the paper for Ms. Adams?"

"Yeah . . ." I stretch my arms over my head to elongate my body. I see Alyssa do it a lot during pageants when she's tired. Every guy within a twenty-foot radius can't help but stare at her, much to the chagrin of the pageant moms. But Grant turns back to Josh to talk about sports.

I decide to up the flirting. I take a piece of paper from my pocket and throw it on the ground. "Oops," I say as I turn so my back is facing them and bend down to grab it. I do it slowly, so he has time to fully get the effect of my butt.

I pause for a few seconds to make sure he had plenty of time to get a good look. I turn around . . . to find that Grant and Josh have left.

"Where did they . . . ?" I say to a stunned Benny. "What happened?"

"Yeah, that was real helpful, Lex," he says dryly. "They left the second your back was turned. Was that even serious?"

"Did you not just see me flirting with him?"

"Is that what that was?" He nudges me playfully.

"Please, he just can't handle my sweet moves." I'm refusing to let Benny know how completely horrified I am right now. I grab his hand as we head to class. "I'm sure Grant's totally picking out an engagement ring right now."

Or a straitjacket.

I get to thinking on my way to lunch that, yes, I did humiliate myself in front of Grant and Josh, but I survived it. I haven't really heard any murmurings about my mental health as I've walked down the hallways between classes. And so what if they think I'm crazy? What's the worst thing that could happen?

I see Hannah and Brooke ahead of me.

"Hey, guys!" I say enthusiastically as we enter the cafeteria. I don't know why I have this rush of confidence, but I want Benny to see me talking to people that I'm not used to hanging out with. Maybe then he'll have the confidence to simply say hi to Chris. That's all I'm asking for. One "hi," no butt-in-the-air required.

"Oh, hey," Hannah replies before looking away from me.

Hannah's father works at the SuperStore with my mom. While my mother works the customer-service desk, he's a senior vice president at the corporate office. Needless to say, they do not run in the same circles.

"Did you have a good weekend?" I ask loudly.

Hannah turns around to make sure that I'm still speaking to her. "Yeah, I guess."

Brooke sticks her slim hip out and impatiently taps her fingers against her lunch tray, which has a bottle of water and a banana on it.

"Did you have fun at Josh's party?" I ask.

They both exchange looks, probably forgetting that they mentioned they were going fourteen times while I was waiting on them at The Cellar.

"It was fun. I posted some pictures on my profile if you want to see them," Hannah offers, probably not sure what else to say.

Brooke looks at me without an ounce of interest. I believe "dead eyes" would be the best description. "Yeah, then you can pretend that you were there." She turns on her heel.

Hannah opens her mouth, but decides against saying anything else. She gives me a little shrug and heads to the table with the Chosen Ones.

Cam has her eyebrow raised as I approach the table in the corner that she, Benny, and I have sat at every semester. "Why were you talking to Hannah and Brooke?" she asks.

I look at Benny. "To prove that you can talk to someone and it won't kill you."

Benny ignores me and continues to eat his fruit salad.

And then I see him. Chris. Walking into the cafeteria.

"There he is." I motion toward the front of the room.

Benny glances up briefly.

"You have to say hi to him. You promised."

He hesitates. "Okay, I'll say hi. But if I do, you have to wear makeup tomorrow to school. And lip balm doesn't count. I want mascara, eye shadow."

He's still on this?

"Fine. But if you want mascara, I want a full-blown conversation. At least two questions."

"I'll do three questions if you wear your hair down," he counters.

Cam keeps looking between the two of us like we're speaking a foreign language.

"Fine." I gesture my hand in Chris's direction. "Go on."

"Now?" Benny's eyes are wide with horror.

"Yes, now!"

He shakes his head. "Can't I at least wait until we're done with lunch? I don't want to go over there and interrupt him. As soon as he stands up and leaves for his locker, I'll do it."

"Okay." He has a point. Plus, this way I can walk behind him and make sure he keeps up with his end of the bargain.

"Can someone tell me what's going on?" Cam finally asks.

We fill Cam in on our negotiations. She stays silent for a little bit afterward. I've been secretly hoping she'd take my side in all of this. I don't really see why I need to put makeup on. It's not like I'm going to magically become a beauty queen and all my problems will just fade away. At least if Benny talks to Chris, it will be a beacon of hope, something for him to hold on to until we can finally get out of this town.

"Don't you think Lexi would look hot if she got all dolled up?" Benny asks Cam.

"Did you just say 'dolled up'?" I tease him.

Cam shrugs her shoulders. "Yeah, I'm sure Lexi would look good with makeup on, but she's also gorgeous as is."

"That's not what I meant," Benny says defensively. "I'm just saying that she believes this nonsense that she's not pretty. So she goes out of her way to live up to this stereotype that's only in her head."

"I'm right here," I feel the need to remind him.

"I know. You're gorgeous, Lexi, you are. I hate that you've let other people's opinions influence what you think about yourself. Especially when those people are delusional."

"So you're basically saying that if I put some lipstick on, I'll suddenly become this super-happy person who'll get loads of dates." *And he thinks other people are delusional?*

"No, that's not . . ." Benny stammers. "I meant . . ."

"Let's just drop it," I say coldly. "I'll wear makeup to school tomorrow. The sun will set and we'll all go on with our lives."

Silence falls on the table. I know both of them are only trying to help, but when I spend every weekend surrounded by some of the most beautiful girls in the state of Texas, I know better than anyone that a little eye shadow isn't going to make much of a difference in my life.

I hear a small noise escape Benny's mouth. I look up to see Chris walking with his empty tray over to the counter, which means he'll have to walk right by us.

"Just do it," I encourage him. "Don't think, do."

His face has gone completely white. But he stands up warily.

Chris sees Benny as he walks by and gives him a slight smile. "Hey, Benny."

He knows his name!

"Hey," Benny says pretty casually (although I know he has to be dying inside).

He walks with Chris, and Cam and I get up to trail behind when I see Taylor Riggins approaching me, waving. I look behind me. Clearly he couldn't be looking for me.

Unless he's heard about my hot flirtatious moves and wants a piece.

Yeah, right.

"Just the person I was looking for." Taylor smiles at me.

I steal a look at Cam, who shrugs her shoulders and takes off after Benny.

"What's up?" I ask.

"So, my mom wants me to get some new clothes for college visits, and I figured we'd go to The Cellar when you were working to make it less painful on me."

"Oh." Of course he wants something from me. Why else would someone like Taylor talk to me? He's gorgeous with a tall, lean build and emerald-green eyes. He's popular, on the football team (although in Texas, one of the requirements to being popular is to BE on the football team). He could only be coming to me for help with his wardrobe.

"Great. So when are you working?" He reaches into his bag and pulls out his phone.

"Tomorrow night from six until close, and then all day Sunday."

"Okay." He runs his fingers through his shaggy brown hair. "I guess we'll come tomorrow."

"Sounds great." At least I know I'll have one good sale.

"All right!" He lifts his hand up for me to give him a high five. I oblige and notice Benny in the corner.

"What happened?" I ask when I get over to him.

"Oh, you know, nothing really . . ." He acts coy. "Chris and I talked and he said he'd save a seat for me in study hall!" He has the biggest grin on his face.

"That's awesome!"

"I know!" He gives me a hug. "Now what were *you* doing talking to Taylor 'überhot' Riggins?"

"Don't get excited." Really, Benny should know better. "He wanted to know when I'm working next so he can come get some new clothes. So he's coming to the store with his mom tomorrow night. No biggy."

Benny gives me a mischievous look. "I've changed my mind — you don't have to get *dolled up* for school tomorrow."

"Thank God."

"Instead, you have to do it for *work* tomorrow."

"Are you kidding me?" I think this might be even worse. Does Benny expect that I'll throw on some mascara and suddenly Taylor will fall for me?

"Stop it. *If* you wore more revealing clothing, then maybe you'd feel sexier," Benny says with a crooked smile.

"*If* Taylor and I were the only people left on earth and the sole hope for survival of the human race was for us to hook up, well, unfortunately it would be the end of humankind as we know it."

Benny leans in so he's only inches away from me. "*If* you started to see yourself the way that we see you, you'd know no one could resist you."

"*If* Taylor had to choose between seven minutes in a closet with me or a gaggle of hungry zombies, I'm sure he'd at least ask me to be the timekeeper for his zombie fight."

"Ugh," Benny groans. "Okay, I get it, I get it. So, what are you going to wear tomorrow night?"

8.

Primpin' Ain't Easy

Mackenzie's makeup kit is essentially a giant toolbox that's bright pink with *Princess* and *Mackenzie* stickers all over it. I open it up and start setting out the items I need for tonight.

I already have my hair in rollers and my Benny-approved outfit on my bed. I'm required to wear at least one item from The Cellar when I'm at work. Luckily, their jeans fit me well, so I'm going to wear those, and a long blue tank over a gray tank with a big belt. I have to admit, it was fun picking out a cute outfit for tonight, deciding to highlight my figure instead of concealing myself. I've been in a personal funk for so long, maybe Benny's right, maybe it's time to get back to the person I was *before*.

My mind wanders back to when I first became interested in clothes. I was five when I started drawing my own designs for outfits. I'd just gotten my first Barbie doll. I'd take wrapping paper, or newspaper as a last resort, and cut out outfits for her. It started simple enough, with a tube dress. Then I moved to more intricate designs (I still have this Oscar-red-carpet-worthy dress I made when I was ten out of shiny red wrapping paper. I spent hours on this floral design that weaved from around the top of the dress to the bottom. Once I finished with it, I knew that I couldn't play with that Barbie any longer. I had to pre-serve her.)

I've seen Mac get her hair and makeup done countless times. Usually, if she's in a grumpy mood, I have to hold her hand or play a game with her so she'll sit still. So I think I know what to do. At least I should be able to put on some mascara and eye shadow: How hard could it pos-sibly be?

I open up the foundation, place it on a sponge, and start to apply. Mac's skin is a little darker than mine, but I think this should look good; it makes me look like I've gotten some sun. I reach in and grab the darker blush, since I'll need it to be brighter to stand out with my now-darker skin tone.

Then I begin working on my eyes. She doesn't have neutral colors, so I decide to try blue to match my tank. I line my eyes with dark navy, and then use a lighter color on my eyelids. I use a few coats of mascara, but poke myself in my right eye with the wand. As I blink, trying to recover from getting black junk in my eyes, tears start to form.

I run over and get a tissue to try to stop the makeup from smearing.

The timer sounds, letting me know I'm supposed to take the rollers out. I start to unravel the rollers from my hair and notice that my hair has formed into tight ringlets. I bend over and try to shake out my hair to get it to calm down. It won't budge. I guess I now know how much hairspray is too much.

I step away from the counter and study myself in the mirror.

My hair, which I wanted to be in loose waves, looks like my muse was a deranged Shirley Temple–like zombie. *Maybe if I brush it out*, I think. I grab a comb and can't even get it through my hair. *Okay, it should calm down after a while.* Or at least I hope.

I finally step back to study my entire face and realize I look like I've come out of three rounds of a heavyweight championship boxing match. The blue makes my eyes looked bruised and my right eye is red from the unfortunate stabbing of the mascara wand.

This is a disaster. Why did I think blue eye shadow would look good on me? I guess the real question is: Why did Benny think that all it would take to transform me into a Glamour Girl was a little makeup? What a joke. But not the funny, ha-ha kind of joke, the what-on-earth-possessed-you-to-be-so-stupid kind.

I glance at the clock and see that I only have twenty minutes before I have to leave for work. I cannot be seen in public like this.

I turn the faucet on and start washing my face. Even soap isn't getting this stuff off. My once-white washcloth is now beige and blue. I turn to Mac's kit for industrial-strength makeup remover.

After five minutes, my face is finally clean. I grab my hair and try to tame it into a ponytail, but it isn't budging. I don't have time to wash it. I grab a few clips to at least get it to settle down. I throw open my closet and grab last season's fedora hat that was all the rage at The Cellar. At least my manager will be excited to see me wearing two Cellar items today.

So much for my bet. I shrug, grab some blush and lip gloss, and hope I didn't just give myself pinkeye.

As I open the bathroom door, I hear a strange noise coming from the living room. I freeze when I realize that it's Mom crying.

I gingerly tiptoe into the room and see her slouched over her desk.

"Mom?" I say quietly.

She jerks herself upright and automatically starts wiping away the tears. "Oh, I thought you were at work." I notice that she's rearranging a stack of bills like they're a deck of cards.

"Is everything okay?"

"Fine." She waves her hand at me dismissively. "Just a long day at work. Nothing to worry about."

But I know there *is* something to worry about, and it's been something we've had hanging over us for years. The pageant spending is getting out of control.

I rack my brain trying to think of something that I can say that won't lead to a fight. What I really want to say is, *Stop doing pageants!*

Mom turns around and looks at me. I'm expecting her to open up, to finally admit that it's gotten to be too much. That she can't keep going on like this.

"Aren't you going to be late for work?" She turns her back on me and picks up a piece of paper to read.

I stand there for another beat before I head out. I don't know why I thought that she'd make any kind of admission to me. Or that she isn't in denial.

I guess it runs in the family.

I'm more grateful than ever to have the distraction of work. Folding and refolding clothes can be therapeutically mind-numbing.

"I knew it!" I hear Benny's voice from behind me. I turn around to see him looking me up and down, shaking his head. "You promised."

"Hear me out . . ." I lead him over to the shirts and start holding up different options for him to look at. The Cellar has a very strict no loitering policy. Benny comes in often to visit me and I make him try on stuff since I'm usually bored. Benny doesn't really like the clothes here; they're too "generic" for his liking.

"We had a deal." He looks disappointed.

"Yeah, we did, but I'm a complete novice and couldn't handle a simple task of putting on mascara or doing my hair." I take off my hat to show Benny the rat's nest that currently resides on top of my head.

"What did you do?" he says incredulously as he touches my hair. "It feels like *straw*."

"Yeah, I had some issues." I shrug my shoulders.

"Well, this doesn't count. You have to try it again."

"Why?" I ask. "You're talking to Chris, so pretty much we both got what we wanted."

Benny looks disappointed. "Not really."

I groan. "Benny, you're talking to him. It's a start. What else do you want?" I hand him a T-shirt to look at as my boss, Mark, starts circling us.

He holds up the shirt and says to it, "For you to become the person you deserve to be."

Seriously? He needs to drop this already.

"I can't really talk right now." I start randomly picking clothes up and straightening them. "I tried it. Epic fail. I'm not meant to be that kind of girl."

"You could ask for help?"

"Who can I ask? My *mother*?" I shake my head. "Not going to happen."

Benny continues to follow me around the store. "Oh, I don't know. What about the hundreds of people at the beauty pageants you go to every weekend?"

"Are you for real?" But I can tell by the look on his face that he is. And he's not going to leave me alone until I give in. "Fine. I'll ask this weekend and I'll wear makeup to school on Monday."

"I want the full week."

"What?"

"The full week."

"Ahem." I hear Mark clear his voice and know I'm going to get in trouble if Benny doesn't leave soon.

"Okay, fine, fine," I say as I usher him out. Maybe once he sees me in hair and makeup he'll realize that nothing is going to change for me. And if it did, how completely shallow are the people at our school? I know looks matter — I'd be an idiot to think they don't — but there are some people who are born beautiful, like Mackenzie, and others who are born to serve the Chosen Ones.

The next couple of hours drag on. The store's dead. I'm now on the floor trying to make sense of the mess that used to be the boot-cut jean display. None of the sizes are together, so I spend the better part of my shift trying to put them in order. It's busy work, but I enjoy it. I feel accomplished after getting everything in nice, orderly fashion . . . only for it to be destroy two seconds later.

"Excuse me, miss?" I recognize Taylor's voice behind me.

I turn around and gesture to the store. "Well, hello, sir. Welcome to The Cellar. How may I help you today?"

"Wow, so professional." He reaches out his hand to help me off the floor.

"Well, The Cellar is not your average clothing-store chain. We're here to make dreams happen. Tell me — wait, don't. I'm getting something."

Taylor laughs as I walk around him, tapping my finger on my lips.

"Yes, I'm sensing a great academic journey coming up. May I suggest our tailored, straight-fit khaki?"

"Sign me up!"

I lead Taylor over to our men's section, ask his size, and start piling different shirts and pants into his arms.

"I didn't realize you were so bossy," he says as I put another shirt in his stack.

"Not bossy, just really good at my job." I lead him toward the dressing room. "I'll be waiting here for the fashion show. Hurry it up."

"Okay, man, you're fast. I'm hoping we can be done with this by the time my mom comes. She spends forever looking at every single item of clothing. If shopping were an endurance sport, she'd be a world-record holder."

I go into the empty dressing rooms and start cleaning up. Taylor comes out in a pair of khakis and a dark-blue-and-white-checkered shirt that's buttoned up all the way to the top.

"What?" He can probably tell from my shaking head that he's done something wrong.

"You've got to loosen up." I unbutton the cuffs of the shirt and begin to fold them up three times. Then I unbutton two buttons at the front.

"Are you undressing me?" Taylor raises his eyebrow.

"In your dreams." I stand back and gesture for him to turn around.

Taylor obliges and twirls around a few times. "I'm kinda feeling like a piece of meat here."

"Shut it and pose for me, model boy." I shake my head. "It's not quite right. Button up your collar — I'll be right back." I run and grab a few ties. "Here." I put the tie around him and start to tie it.

"You know how to tie a tie?" He seems impressed.

"Yep." *No thanks to my dad.*

"There you are!" Taylor's mom walks in, her hands full of shopping bags from all the pricey stores in the mall. "Oh, doesn't that look nice?" Mrs. Riggins makes Taylor turn around for her. "Well done, Lexi."

"Thanks. What I was thinking is that he could wear this during the campus tours and then . . ." I go into his dressing room and pull out a matching blazer. I hand it to Taylor to put on. "He can put this on for the interview. If it's cooler out, he can wear a sweater vest over it."

"I'm so not wearing a sweater vest," Taylor objects.

Mrs. Riggins nods to herself. "Try one on anyway."

Taylor sulks and goes into the dressing room to put on the vest I pulled for him.

"See, that's not so bad," Mrs. Riggins says when her not-amused son returns.

Taylor steps back and looks in the mirror. "Hey, this actually looks pretty cool. I look like I belong in, like, GQ or something." He then poses like he's looking at his watch, then puts his hand on his chin like he's in deep thought.

"I put together a few other color combinations as well, sticking with the basic colors, figuring Taylor wouldn't be caught dead in a peach."

"Good call."

Mrs. Riggins smiles warmly at me. "We'll take it all. Thanks so much, Lexi."

"Of course."

She follows me to the cash register. I start ringing up what will most likely be my biggest sale of the week, if not the month. She hasn't once looked at a price tag.

"How are things with your family?" she asks.

I do my best to smile. "Great."

"And your sister? Are things going well on the pageant circuit for her?"

Since I spend so much time talking about pageants at home, I usually try to avoid the topic when I'm at work or school. But I give her a big wide smile. "Wonderful. She was crowned Princess last week, and we've got another pageant this weekend."

"That's wonderful." She pulls out a platinum credit card. "She came by Taylor's dad's office a few weeks ago for some kind of fundraising."

No. Please no.

I specifically asked Mom that anybody associated with me not be put in an awkward position of giving Team Mackenzie money.

"Stewart showed me the picture he got of your sister. She looked like a little cowgirl."

Dear God, not western wear. Please don't tell me that Mom took Mackenzie around town dressed up like a cowgirl to beg for money.

"I had no idea those pageants cost so much."

Oh, they do. They cost so much money, time, effort, dignity. . . .

I smile and nod as I tally up Taylor's five shirts, three pants, two ties, two blazers, and one sweater vest. The cost doesn't even match that of Mackenzie's beauty gown, one that she'll wear only a few times because she'll either grow out of it or Mom will feel the need to compete with the girls with more money who wear new gowns every time.

I try to go through the paces and not die of humiliation right here and now.

I'm fine being part of Team Mackenzie on the weekends and during the week. But I wanted to have somewhere that was just for me, even if that place is work. Everybody deserves a respite from pageants.

But I guess I don't get one.

9.

Hair Extensions and Fake Eyelashes: That's What Pretty Girls Are Made Of

*T*here's trouble afoot at Princess Central.

Mom's rummaging through her "emergency supply" crate, which contains everything from spot remover, scissors, and bleach to sugar sticks, an energy drink that contains five times the caffeine of a regular soda, and, what Mom really needs right now, antacid. But that's not what she's looking for.

"There's got to be something here to help." She starts grabbing at her hair. Her cheeks flush more than usual.

She turns to Mackenzie, her eyes pleading. "Please, baby, try it one more time."

Mom delicately hands Mac her flipper, a necessity in the glitz pageant world. Flippers are basically dentures for tots — fake teeth to cover up Mac's missing teeth and gaps *because she's seven*. She's not supposed to have perfect pearly whites, but 'tis the law of glitz.

Mac puts the flipper in. She smiles and my little sister has these huge horselike teeth that look so unnatural.

Mom collapses on the hotel bed in relief.

Mac goes to say something, but the flipper falls out.

"NO!" Mom turns over on the bed.

There's a knock on the door. Sensing that Mom's not capable of having any kind of human interaction at this point, I get up and let in Lauren, Mac's hair-and-makeup person.

"Hey, y'all!" Lauren gives me a little squeeze on the shoulder. I don't understand how she does what she does every weekend. She travels to these pageants and spends all morning primping kids. Between the demanding mothers and fidgeting divas, I seriously can't believe she hasn't gone postal. She once explained to me that she makes more money in one day at a pageant than she does in an entire week at the salon she works for. She's saving up for a house, and once that's done she's going to retire from pageants. While I'm happy for her, she's really the only person in the entire pageant world that Mackenzie consistently behaves for. So once she's gone, Hurricane Mac will be unstoppable.

"Hi, Miss Lauren!" Mac coos sweetly to her.

"Well, hello, Miss Mackenzie!" Lauren lifts her suitcase and begins to take out all her tools. "You seem to be in a good mood this early morning. What's going on with your mama?" Lauren tilts her head toward Mom, who now has a pillow covering her head.

"My flipper isn't staying in." Mackenzie hands it over like Lauren won't be disgusted by the fact that it was just in Mac's mouth.

Lauren kneels down. "Well, let's see what we can do, shall we?" She puts the flipper in Mac's mouth. "Smile for me."

Mac obliges.

"Well, isn't that the most gorgeous set of teeth you've ever seen?"

Not really.

Mac beams at Miss Lauren. She then goes to laugh, but the flipper falls out. For a split second, she looks like an elderly person who's lost her dentures.

"Oh, I see." Miss Lauren puts the flipper back in. "Well, hon, I guess you're just going to have to keep your teeth closed when you're up on stage. You can do that, can't you?"

Mac nods.

Crisis averted.

Mom finally gets up off the bed. "Thanks so much, Miss Lauren."

It's business as usual as Lauren starts rolling Mac's hair in curlers. I get back to glitzing up Mac's T-shirt for crowning. All the contestants received a "free" Miss Cutie Pie (or whatever today's pageant is) T-shirt upon check-in. Of course we had to pay over three hundred dollars to enter, so not really sure what's so free about it. It's my job to glam it up, so I'm currently adding pink ribbon and rhinestones. It's not the kind of fashion that I aspire to, but it keeps the peace.

Mom starts examining Lauren's work curling Mac's fall (her hairpiece), yet another requirement of glitz pageants: big hair. "Miss Lauren, have you seen what some of those moms have been saying online about the girls?"

Lauren stays focused. "No, ma'am, I haven't. I think it's best to stay away from those things."

"Well, it's awful." Mom starts wiping her brow and I can tell she's ready to go into a tirade. "Some of these mothers are disgusting. There's a certain group of women, and I will not name names, but they have been ganging up on some of the girls, calling them names. They're only kids. I went right on there, I did, and I said, 'You watch what you're sayin' because you don't know if the judges are on there, and you can call me what you want, but you don't make fun of my child.'" Mom fervently nods in agreement with herself.

Mac yawns. "What did they say, Mama? Did they say something about me?"

I shoot Mom a warning glance. Mac has many years ahead of her where she'll have to deal with bullies, on- and offline. I'm hoping Mom will let her be a kid, even if she's currently getting fake hair pinned to her head.

"Nothing, sweetheart." Mom hovers closely over Lauren. "I want to make sure her hair is *big*. I want *big* curls. Last pageant, Holli Cooper had this gorgeous fall. There's no way her color is real, is it?"

Miss Lauren smiles politely. "Holli's a beautiful girl, just like Mackenzie. Should be a good competition today."

Mom starts pacing the room, unhappy not to get any intel on Mac's biggest competition. Holli Cooper's beaten Mackenzie, and pretty much their entire age group, at every competition for the last year. She has this fiery red hair that really makes her stand out. And Mom has been desperate to find out if her hair color's real. It's funny that she would think that would make a difference. Glitz essentially means *go big or go home*. The contestants have to do everything to stand out: spray tans, expensive dresses, professionally choreographed routines, you name it. It's not like it would make any difference if Holli's hair came in a bottle.

Mackenzie starts getting antsy, which is completely understandable since she's been sitting in that chair for over an hour. That's difficult at any age. And it probably doesn't help that she had a Cherry Coke and a chocolate donut for breakfast.

"You want your special juice?" Mom asks Mac.

I literally bite my tongue as Mom gives Mac an energy drink. I once decided to taste it and it was disgusting. There's no way something that people drink at raves is good for a seven-year-old. But they practically sell the stuff in bulk on days like today. I guess I should be grateful Mom hasn't busted out the sugar sticks. It's only a little after eight in the morning, after all. Straight sugar is usually given right before the talent competition.

Lauren applies the final touches on Mackenzie. I figure I can make my move while Mom is busying oohing and aahing over Mac.

I approach Lauren cautiously.

"Well, Miss Lexi, I have to say, I love your outfit." Lauren looks down at my new cami and fitted jeans with knee-high boots. This is probably the first time she's seen me in anything but a baggy Mackenzie T-shirt. I decided to take baby steps and wear something new and better fitting today. I even caught the bellhop checking me out, and it felt nice.

I need to stop fighting my desire to dress up in nice, cute clothing. I'd like to say I forgot why I stopped doing it in the first place, but I'm not that good of a liar, especially to myself.

"Thanks." I lower my voice. "Um, could I talk to you later, when you have a free moment?"

I know Lauren's schedule is packed, but Benny's right. In order to avoid another Clown Face Incident, I need professional help. And while it's seriously possible that I might need a therapist's help after this is all over, right now I need a hair-and-makeup stylist.

"Of course. Come find me in the all-purpose room during talent. I should be mostly done by then."

I thank Lauren, grateful that Mom and Mac have no idea what I'm up to. Although truthfully, I don't think Mom could even see me any other way than she sees me as her dependable daughter. The work-horse. The student. The responsible one.

Mackenzie's the pretty one.

I slip out to find Lauren once talent starts. I've seen Mac's various dance routines so many times that I could perform them in my sleep. Today's one of my favorites: Mac dresses up as a teacher and dances to the Jackson 5's "ABC." It's pretty adorable, even if her pageant version of a teacher wears a spandex-and-rhinestone hot pants suit.

The conference room next to the pageant looks like it's been destroyed. Chairs are overturned, empty garment bags and accessories litter the floor. I see Lauren talking with a few other stylists. A lot of the pageant girls use this room to get ready, but Mom usually insists on getting her own room, which adds another $200 to the bill for today. With everything for today's pageant, I'm pretty sure Mom's spent nearly $1,500 . . . and the top prize is only $200.

"Well, hello there, Miss Lexi." Lauren gives me a hug. "Been a long day, huh?" I smile politely. "What can I do for you?"

"I know you must be exhausted and you've been working all day, but I was wondering if I could ask you some questions . . . about hair and makeup?"

Lauren's face lights up. "Of course! You know, I've been dying to get my hands on your cheekbones." She leads me to a chair.

"Oh, I don't want you to feel like you need to give me a makeover or anything. It's just, I tried to put makeup on the other day, and I've been watching people do it to Mackenzie for years, but when I did it, I looked like a —"

Lauren laughs. "Oh, honey, glitz makeup's not meant to be worn out in public. Or I guess I should say it *shouldn't* be worn out in public. Look at Alyssa. You've seen her at school. Does she look anything like the Alyssa you saw on stage today?"

True, Alyssa doesn't wear as much makeup as she does on stage, but she still looks gorgeous. Just ask Logan.

"Oh my goodness." Lauren shakes her head. "I can only image what you would've looked like trying to use Mackenzie's makeup. But do not worry your pretty little head, we can do something without making you look like a two-dollar streetwalker."

"Yeah, I'd prefer to look like a ten-dollar one. I do have standards."

Lauren's laugh fills the room. "Oh, sweetie, you're too much. Plus, you and Mackenzie have totally different coloring. She has an olive complexion and you're paler with a reddish undertone that a little concealer can help even out." She starts putting a cream on my face. "To be honest — and please do not take this the wrong way — I've been wanting to do your eyebrows for months." She runs her fingers across my eyebrows. "They're gorgeous, but need a little bit of taming. Do you mind?" She lifts up a pair of tweezers.

I nod my head and close my eyes. I try to go to a happy place as I feel the hairs being ripped out one by one. Whoever said "beauty is pain" is right. I need to give Mackenzie more credit. Yes, she's only seven, but that doesn't stop Mom from having her eyebrows waxed before a big pageant. I refuse to make any noise, but I feel tears start forming in my eyes.

Just when I'm about ready to scream "uncle," Lauren puts a cooling liquid on my eyebrows. "See, all better. Your eyes pop more."

It's amazing what a little grooming can do. My face already looks a ton better . . . except for the red splotches from the plucking.

I start making a list of items to buy and take diligent notes on what Lauren's doing with her makeup tools and curling iron.

She gives me a satisfied smile when she's finished. She holds up a mirror for me to study the final look. It's amazing. I look like me, just a better version. And she made it look more natural than I thought. You can't really tell I have a bunch of makeup on, and that's what I wanted. My hair is probably the biggest difference. She used a curling iron to give my normally limp hair some much needed body and wave.

A text from Benny appears on my phone:

Chris just txted me!!!! What do I get if I reply to him and ask him 2 do something?

I get so excited for Benny. I reply back:

A date?

Haha. I want leg.

???

I want you to show some leg on Mon. And not long dress, above the knee.

Perv.

U know me so well!

A makeover *and* a dress? There is a very good chance no one will even recognize me on Monday.

Including myself.

*   *   *

I try to sneak into the room during crowning. On my way in, two people wish me luck. I try not to laugh. I don't look *that* good.

"Let me get this for you." One of the pageant dads holds open the door and smiles at me. Nobody ever smiles at me, or even notices me, at these things. I know I should be flattered, but it sort of annoys me that some makeup and hairspray is all it takes for people to be polite.

Once I get to the room, I look up to the front where Mackenzie and Mom are. They don't even seem to notice that I've been gone for nearly an hour and missed talent and most of the crowning. I see that Mackenzie already has her tiara.

"What'd I miss?" I whisper to Logan.

"Where were you? I've been —" Logan stops himself and squints his eyes at me. "I . . . Are you wearing makeup? Your hair's different, too."

Okay, so I guess when one has never really worn makeup before and one's hair isn't in its usual messy ponytail, it's obvious that something's different.

"It's nothing. Miss Lauren and I were just goofing around."

"Oh, well, you look nice."

I face forward, certain that the foundation I have on will not disguise the heat that I feel rising in my face. I can see Logan stealing glances at me. I can't tell if this is a good thing or a bad thing. Does he think I look good or is he embarrassed on my behalf for me trying to be someone I'm not?

Or does he want to run off into the sunset with me?

Well, it's nice to know that some things never change.

I decide to go for further distraction and reach in my bag for a snack. "Almonds?" I offer.

Logan takes a few. "You're the only person I know at this place who has anything not completely laced with sugar. Even Alyssa, who won't touch it during the week, consumes handfuls of the stuff here. It's weird."

"Yeah, well, have you seen my mother?" I nod my chin toward Mom, who takes up nearly two seats. "Genetics are not on my side."

I feel a pang of guilt that I've said something about my mom's weight. While I know genetics are partially responsible, I also know that she gained over a hundred pounds after Dad left. She stopped taking care of herself, and just kept eating. The only thing that would get her out of her rut was pageants.

I tried to talk to her about it, concerned for her health, but it only made her mad at me. I even went to the school nurse and got some brochures on nutrition that I left out on the kitchen table. I found them in the trash later that night.

I study her now as she walks over to us. I see the looks the other people give her when she passes by. It's not only the children that are being judged today.

And while I admit that my mom's weight sometimes embarrasses me, I'm more upset by a greater offense: her complete lack of concern over her health.

The way she appears to have given up.

10.

Flippers — They're Not Just for Dolphins Anymore

know how much it costs to be pageant pretty. But real-life pretty isn't much better.

I stare down at the receipt from my shopping trip after work, grateful that I'm good about saving money. After all, I don't really have much of a social life, so there's no need to spend a lot of cash. Hanging out at Benny's to watch movies on a Friday night is cheap. Plus, I'm saving for this summer in New York. I have a little satisfaction every time I go to the bank and see my growing balance. It makes me feel like I'm accomplishing something.

But while I'm scraping together every penny, Mom keeps spending.

After seeing Mom cry last week, there's a part of me that wants to help her, help Mac. But I figure someone in this family needs to be the fiscally responsible one.

Hence, the current argument.

"Do you have any idea how long it takes me to save up five hundred dollars — and you want me to give it to you for fake teeth?" I shove the drug store receipt farther into my back pocket. If she knew that I just spent a bunch of money to try to make *me* look pretty, she'd lose it. A pang of guilt erupts inside me over the money that I spent, but I never spend money (that I *earned*) on myself.

Mom glares at me. "I'm well aware how long it takes to get that kind of money, but the old flippers don't work anymore and we can't do glitz pageants without them. It's not like we won't pay you back when she wins."

Mackenzie finally perks up. "No! That's my money."

I don't even see why we're having this conversation since Mackenzie never earns back the money. I once did some estimating, and she's earned about seven hundred dollars over the last five years. Which wouldn't seem so bad if we haven't spent *tens of thousands* of dollars on pageants.

"You're right, honey — it's your money." Mom brushes Mackenzie's hair out of her face. Then she turns back to me. "I *promise* I'll pay you back when I get the money." Mom holds her hand up like she's swearing in at a trial.

"Just like you did with the money I lent you for Mac's new photos?" I counter. Last year I *lent* them over two hundred fifty dollars to get new head shots. After three months I stopped asking for it back.

"You're being incredibly selfish, Lexi."

As if on cue, Mackenzie starts crying. A horrible, high-pitched sob, complete with a scrunched-up face. She stomps on the floor.

"Oh, honey." Mom motions for Mac to come and give her a hug.

"NO!" Mac yells and runs to her room, slamming the door nice and loud.

I look at the closed door. "That went well. . . ."

"Oh hush, Lexi. This isn't funny, and you're not helping any."

I'm afraid to try to talk to her again about it, but I can tell from Mom's haggard expression that things are pretty dire. "How bad is it?"

"Well, it's not good." She shakes her head. And for a brief moment, I think Mom's finally going to admit that we're in over our heads. "I think we have a real shot next weekend, but not if we don't have a new flipper."

How naïve of me to think that she'd ever admit there are any problems in the perfect Mackenzie world she's created in her mind.

"And there's something else." She reaches into her bag and pulls out a questionnaire. I see the *Texas Beauty Tykes* logo across the top.

"Please don't tell me you want to be on that show?"

Texas Beauty Tykes is a "reality" television show that showcases one "junior" Texas beauty queen pageant contestant each week. Most of the time the kid and her family come across as completely insane.

Usually people blame editing, but I've seen some of the families in real life, and I truly believe the editors were trying to make them look good.

"Can you imagine the exposure it would get Mac? It could really take her to the next level."

I really want to ask who they've featured in the past that's now a huge star, but I know there's no chance of talking any sense into her.

Mom continues. "The producers are going to be at the Texas Royal Pageant in two weeks, and all we're doing is trying to get an interview. So that's why it's so important for her to have new teeth . . . and a new dress."

I look up at Mom. It's never going to be enough for her. That's how I know that if I give her that money, I'll never get it back. There will always be another thing we need. There'll always . . . *Wait*. Something registers in my head.

"Next weekend? That's when we're supposed to go see Dad."

Two years after the divorce, Dad moved to a Houston suburb for a new position within his accounting firm. Mackenzie and I get to see him two weekends a month — or I should say we're *supposed* to see him two weekends a month. Usually a pageant gets in the way. Even though a lot of the pageants are in the Houston area, we still don't get to see him because we're too busy with the pageants, and he doesn't want to have anything to do with them.

With all the distractions, I haven't been able to see my own father in nearly two months. And I guess what hurts the most is that he hasn't fought it. Mom always talks about how these pageants are what "we" want to do, as if Mac and I don't want to see our own father. I miss my father so much it aches inside. He gets me. He gets how ridiculous the whole pageant scene is.

I don't care what Mom says, I'm still going.

Mom waves dismissively at me. "I know it's your weekend with your father. I already took care of it."

"What do you mean you *took care of it?*"

"I called him and told him we'd have to reschedule."

"You did what?"

Mom rubs her temples. "You know, Lexi, I've had just about enough of you."

I feel something in me snap. "You know what, *Mom*. I've had enough of *you*! How dare you cancel our weekend with Dad without consulting us first."

Mom's voice rises. "I don't need to consult you. *I'm* your mother — don't you forget that."

I feel so much anger bubbling inside of me. I spend so much time doing what they want, what needs to be done for the pageant, what about what *I* want?

"Why can't I go without Mackenzie?" I plead. "You don't *need* me at the pageant. Plus, I can't keep switching my work schedule around. Mark is already annoyed that I had to cancel another weekend, because it's not like weekends are busy at the mall or anything. But I guess none of this matters. No, of course not, because the entire world revolves around your precious *favorite* daughter!"

I don't even let her respond. I run to my room and slam the door shut, just like Mackenzie. Maybe if I start *acting* like her, I can start getting a vote around here.

11.

Glitz Me Baby, One More Time

*W*hile I wasn't thrilled when my alarm woke me up two hours earlier than normal on a school day, things are going pretty well. I spent all day yesterday giving myself a manicure and pedicure. (All I have to say is that I'm very thankful for the invention of nail polish remover.) I also applied tanning lotion to my arms and legs, using the lightest color so it wouldn't be so obvious. I have to admit, it really makes my skin tone look a little less *Night of the Living Dead*.

And, yes, I'm wearing a dress.

I put the last finishing touches on my outfit and examine myself in the mirror. This time I was able to actually make my hair have natural-looking waves, although there's so much product in my hair, there ain't nothing natural about it. I gave myself smoky eyes, used one of Lauren's many tricks to make my eyelashes look about twenty times bigger than they actually are, and applied a little bit of shimmer to my exposed arms and legs to give me a little glow.

I'll just go ahead and say it: I don't look half bad. I didn't do as nice of a job as Miss Lauren, but for a complete novice, I really can't complain.

I know there's no way that I'll ever be able to top this, so I hope that Benny doesn't figure out a way to get me to wear an actual pageant gown to school. Because if he wants that, he's taking Chris to prom.

I wish I could go right to school to see Benny's reaction, but first I have to face my harshest critics.

"Good morning," I say as I reach in the refrigerator for some juice.

I turn around to see both Mom and Mackenzie staring at me with their mouths agape.

"Lexi? Is that a *dress*?" Mom looks me up and down as if she can't recognize an item of clothing as familiar as a dress on her oldest child. She comes over to me and puts her hands on my face. "What in the world? What happened to you? You look like a lady."

"Thanks, Mom. Do we have any oranges left?" I reach around the counter, pretending to be busy.

"Is there something special going on at school today?" Mom continues to stare.

"Nope. Just thought I'd try something new for a change."

She smiles at me. "You really look lovely, dear."

"Thanks." We both give each other a little nod. It takes everything I have to not remind her that she didn't think that this would ever be possible. But I don't want to go there today. Today is going to be a happy day.

"Doesn't your sister look beautiful, Mackenzie?" Mom has never used that word to describe me. And as soon as that word escapes her mouth, I realize how much I've been craving it.

"Why does *she* get a new outfit?"

And like that, the moment is ruined.

"Well, I hate to break up the lovefest, but I gotta go." I grab an apple and head to my car. Pretty much the only benefit of being from a broken home is that I have my own car courtesy of Father Guilt.

I look at myself in the rearview mirror. I hardly recognize the person staring back at me, but I can't help but like what I see.

I hate it when Benny's right.

Benny and Cam are waiting for me in the parking lot. The two of them start banging at my car window the second I'm parked and taunt me like a bunch of construction workers to get out.

Once they see me, it takes a couple minutes for the shock to sink in.

"Come here and let me admire my handiwork!" Benny stands back and looks me up and down.

"*Your* handiwork?" I'm annoyed. "You didn't have to get up two hours earlier to make *this* happen!"

He chuckles, but keeps staring at me. "I don't mean to ogle you." Benny's eyes go up and down the new me. "But who knew you had such hot gams?"

"*Gams?*" I tease him. "I know your clothing choices are stuck in the eighties, but didn't realize your vocabulary is from the thirties."

"Hey!" Benny says as he flashes me his *CHiPs* T-shirt. "I'll have you know that Chris finds my taste in clothing, and I quote, 'a-freakin'-dorable.'"

"That's great. So *why* do I have to do this again?" I ask. Part of me feels super shallow for liking this fancy version of myself.

"To prove a point," Benny says with authority.

"What point? That you're a top-notch negotiator?"

He sighs. "No, that you're a total hottie."

I look at Cam for some support, but she's staring down at my high-heeled sandals.

"Don't those hurt?" she asks.

"Beauty is pain." This is today's mantra.

"More like a pain in the butt."

"Tell me about it." A well-timed yawn spreads over me. I was hoping that maybe I could rely on adrenaline to get me through the day, but it looks like I'm not going to be that fortunate.

"Shall we?" Benny holds out his arm for me to take. "I can't wait for all those stupid jocks to see the hottest girl in school on *my* arm." He grabs Cam with his other arm. "Make that the *two* hottest girls."

She nudges Benny playfully. "Nice save."

The three of us walk into school and toward my locker. I didn't really think past seeing Benny and getting through our bet. I'm not really sure what people will think, if they'll even notice.

I'm overly self-conscious as we walk through the hallway. The only thing I can think of is to treat this like Mac handles a runway.

Then it hits me: High school is *exactly* like a beauty pageant.

Of course. Walking down a hallway is like being on stage, being judged by your appearance. Instead of a tiara (unless you're Homecoming or Prom Queen), you're anointed worthy of a spot at the Beautiful People table.

I'd laugh if it weren't so sad. I think back to some of Mom's many tips of navigating the pageant world. Like: *When in doubt, smile.* I decide against the toothy, fake pageant smile and go with a normal, sane-person smile. I notice a few people smile back at me, but without a sense of recognition. I don't know what I was expecting, but I get a few double takes when I turn the corner.

As soon as we reach my locker, I think, *Now what?* Am I really going to have to spend the entire day, not to mention the week, like this? Won't people assume I've lost my mind?

"I guess I should, um, get my things?" It's as if the makeup has made me incapable of understanding how to behave in school.

"Yeah, I've got to head to class," Cam says apologetically, probably sensing my total discomfort. "Good luck."

She gives me a hug before heading off. Benny gives me a huge grin.

I shrug my shoulders at him. "Well, I guess —"

"Oh my God, *Lexi?*"

We turn around to see Alyssa staring at me, her eyes wide.

"Hey, Alyssa." At first I'm confused about her shocked attitude, but then I remember that I look like . . . one of her kind.

She comes over and starts examining me up and down. "I almost didn't recognize you. You look fantastic. What . . ."

"What *happened?*" I finish her thought. Benny has faded into the background; he wants to listen, not participate.

Alyssa's cheeks flush. "I didn't mean it that way. I guess I'm just not used to . . ." She bites her lip. Clearly she knows she's on shaky ground. I'm probably going to get this a lot today: genuine compliments that are barely disguising sheer shock that I could make myself look nice.

I catch Logan out of the corner of my eye. He's walking toward Alyssa, who's busy circling me, complimenting me on everything from the color of my lip gloss to my sandals. I won't pretend like I haven't imagined this scenario a million times in my head: Logan spots me down the hallway and rushes toward me, unable to hide his feelings any longer.

But this is reality, and his eyes are currently fixated on Alyssa.

I realize that I'm literally holding my breath in anticipation.

What if he doesn't notice? What if he doesn't say anything?

Man, you can cover up a lot on a girl, but you can't hide ugly desperation.

"Hey there . . ." Logan lights up as he comes over to give Alyssa a quick kiss. His eyes flicker to me, then back to Alyssa, then . . .

"Lexi?" He looks at Alyssa again.

She's nodding at him to confirm what he's seeing. It's almost like I can hear what she's trying to say to him, *"I know, can you believe it? Lexi's a girl. Who knew?"*

"Hey!" His voice shoots up really high. He clears his throat. "Hey, what's up?"

"Not much." I smile wide at him, almost daring him to pretend like he doesn't notice anything.

"You . . . um," he stammers.

"Doesn't Lexi look *ah*-mazing?" Alyssa practically squeals. Like I'm some new doll she gets to play with.

He nods. "Yeah, you look great. I, um, need to get . . ."

Alyssa looks at the clock. "Yikes! We better get going. And, Lexi, can't wait to talk to you more. You have to teach me how you got your eyelashes so big!"

I give her a smile as she leaves hand in hand with Logan.

"Well, well . . ." Benny reappears with a mischievous smirk on his face. "Is it me, or did you make Logan speechless?"

I hook my arm around Benny's as we head to class, and a surge of confidence overcomes me.

"You know, Benny, I think this is going to be a very good week."

Now I know what it must feel like to be an animal in a zoo. All day people have been studying me in my artificially natural habitat.

I can feel Brooke's eyes burning into the back of my head during trig. I'm trying to write down an equation on the board, but feel like I need to look glamorous doing it. I think back to another pageant tip Mom always gives Mac: *You're always being judged.* I don't know why, but I find myself puckering my lips a bit. What scares me the most is that it's almost an automatic reflex.

The bell rings and I decide not to get up right away, but to wait to see if she'll say something.

She stops in front of me and gives me a little scowl. "Special occasion?"

"Excuse me?" I tilt my head and open my eyes wide to display innocence.

"Why are you dressed . . . up?"

"Just thought I'd try something different." And then to get a sarcastic remark from her, I do a little twirl. "Do you like it?"

She shrugs. "Better than you usually look."

And that, ladies and gentlemen, is probably the best compliment you could hope to receive from Brooke Hanley.

I try to wipe the smile off my face as I walk down the hallway. I see Grant up ahead staring at my legs. I resist the urge to look down and make sure I haven't gotten any dirt on them, although I'm not sure how that would've happened.

By the time Grant's gaze gets up to my face, it's clear there's a bit of confusion as he's trying to place me. He obviously knows who I am, but he isn't sure how. He hits Josh's shoulder to get his attention and points at me. Like, totally pointing at me in the middle of the hallway. Does he not think that I can see him? Does he *want* me to see him?

I do my best not to stare as Josh and Grant exchange a few words.

Gee, wonder who they're talking about?

Grant's eyes get wide as the realization that the girl he was disgusted to even consider going to Homecoming with is the same person whose legs he was just checking out.

I slow my pace slightly as I walk by. I decide to throw him a quick glance over my shoulder, like the ones I've seen flirty girls do on TV. Of course, those girls have extras around them who watch where they're going. I'm not as fortunate and run into someone and nearly fall over in these deathly high heels. I'm sure some people wouldn't consider three-inch heels deathly, but they might as well be ten feet high with my coordination skills.

I steady myself and walk to my next class. Being careful not to let my legs (or imagination) get ahead of me.

My day of feeling overly paranoid increases as Benny and Cam stop what appears to be a heated conversation as soon I sit down for lunch. My stomach has been in constant knots all day. As soon as I get comfortable in class, the bell rings and I have to go back to parading in the hallway.

"What?" I skip pleasantries and get down to business.

Benny shakes his head a little too forcefully. "Nothing. Just talking about English homework."

"It's so obvious when you lie."

He throws his apple down. "Nothing. It's just that I overhead some stuff."

"About me?"

They both stay silent.

"Come on, Benny, you're responsible for all of this." It's clear they're trying to protect me from something, and I want to know what's going on. I figure guilt will work. "You know, it's really great that you're talking to Chris. I don't really see why it's still required for me to be completely humiliated." What's weird is that I haven't really been humiliated today. There's been lots of talk, but nothing bad, *that I'm aware of.*

Cam gives me a slight smile. "Oh, you haven't been humiliated. But you *are* a hot topic of conversation today."

"Is it bad?" Another stomach knot forms. I knew that this was a possibility. It's pretty much what I expected, that people could think that I was a joke.

"Mostly it's all positive, people saying that you look hot. And you know how guys are."

"Actually I don't." I turn toward Benny.

He throws his hands up. "As if *I* know what guys are like. I have no idea if this coffee outing I'm having with Chris is a date or not. And *I'm* a guy. *Please.*"

Cam sighs. "They're all like . . ." Cam makes her voice low, "*'Dude, have you seen Lexi, she's looking hot, wouldn't mind getting me a piece of that.'* You know, stupid guy stuff."

"Really?" I try to not make it known how happy this makes me. "I mean, that's not all that bad, right?"

Benny claps his hands in excitement. "Of course not! This is awesome, Lex. I bet you're going to be asked out on a date before the week is through."

"Really?"

Cam lets out an exasperated sigh. "Do I need to have the boyfriend talk with you again?"

The "boyfriend talk" is one that we've had many times. Usually it involves me feeling sorry for myself, and Cam thinking that I'm being ridiculous because it's the guy's problem if he can't see how awesome I am and love me for me. That it's *his* issue because he can't handle a strong woman who has thoughts and opinions.

I hate that excuse when it comes to my status as Consistently Single. That it's not me. No, of course not. It's apparently every single straight human being on the planet with a Y chromosome.

I always dutifully listen to Cam when she's giving me advice on guys since she has way more experience than me, although that's not hard since I have *zero* experience. Cam even went to Homecoming last year, and Jeremy Wells tried to go to second base with her. Cam, being Cam, got mad.

At this point, I'd like the opportunity to at least go to bat.

Cam takes my silence as an invitation to start in on the talk. "You have to remember that all those TV shows and movies where the girl meets the guy of her dreams at sixteen is bogus. Just like the shows where a girl has a makeover and all her life's problems go away. That's not real life. Guys, and relationships, in high school aren't like that. Let's see, I think the most romantic date I've been on was when Hunter Perkins took me to dinner and accidentally spilled his soda on my white cardigan. He got me club soda to try to soak up the stain, which was conveniently located on my chest, so he was being a *total gentleman* in trying to help me wipe it off. Honestly, that's it. There's been no swelling of music when they try to make a move on you in the backseat of a car or at a dance. You deserve more."

Cam continues, "I just don't understand why someone as awesome as you needs to feel justified by having a guy show interest in you. Plus, what does it say about a guy if he asks you out now because of how you look? All it took is some makeup to be treated the way you should be treated? It's pathetic."

"*Some* makeup? It took me *two hours* to look like this!"

"Exactly." She smiles like she's won another one of her debate team matches.

I guess she's right. But when you've been ignored for as long as I have, you might not mind that this is what it takes to get noticed by a guy. Even if it *is* a little infuriating.

"Okay, okay." I give in. There's no point in arguing with Cam, especially when I know deep down that she's right. I seriously need to get some friends who'll let me be the smart one for a change.

I notice Cam and Benny exchange a look.

Cam bites into her sandwich. "*Anyways*, I'm thinking of going to the bookstore after school if anybody wants to join me."

Wait a second. They both knew that I wouldn't be upset that some guys were saying things about me. Something else is going on. I can tell.

"What aren't you telling me?" I ask firmly.

They look skeptically at each other for a few beats, before Benny gives Cam a small nod.

Cam turns to me. "You know that Brooke is pure evil. Well, she's trying to start some rumor that you had plastic surgery or something. Nobody believes her."

Benny agrees. "Yeah, especially since we all know that plastic surgery would require weeks to heal. I only know that thanks to Brooke and her new nose over summer break. You know how easily she gets threatened because of her status as Queen Glamour Girl."

I guess I should've expected as much from Brooke. It was only a matter of time before she set her sights on me. But I find myself more excited than annoyed by her attempts to defame my makeover.

If I'm doing something to make Brooke nervous enough to spread rumors about me, I must be doing something right.

12.

Popularity Crashers

This week is both exhausting and exhilarating. The tireless hours I spend on "Glam Lexi" aren't fun, but each day at school gets better and better. The whispers turn into actual conversations with people who I didn't even think knew my name.

By Wednesday, Grant has invited me to his party.

I'm almost expecting confetti to explode and a *Congratulations for Finally Being Invited!* banner to drop down from the ceiling when he asks me. I know that's a tad pathetic, but I think it's normal to want (or crave) the acceptance of the Beautiful People. It almost makes me realize what Mac must feel up on stage looking at the judges, wanting so much for them to literally put her on a pedestal.

Oddly enough, the most difficult part about the process of going to said party is not the tireless hours spent primping each morning — it's convincing Benny and Cam to go with me.

"I can't believe we're doing this," Benny says for the twentieth time as we head up the sidewalk to Grant's house on Saturday night.

"We aren't going to let Lexi go alone, and, need I remind you, this is all your doing," Cam says to him, also for the twentieth time.

"Yeah," I agree. "Totally all your fault." I can't hide a smile. "So, how do I look?" I twirl around in my skinny jeans, black fitted tank top, and knee-high boots. I spruced up the outfit with silver bangles and a necklace. I'm wearing my hair in loose waves that took me an hour to create.

"Hot. You look hot," Cam tells me . . . for the twentieth time.

Okay, maybe none of us is really comfortable with this whole Popular Posse Party thing.

"Are you sure they know I'm coming?" Benny asks.

I shrug. "I don't really think Grant is one for formal RSVPs. But there was no way I was going to leave you at home."

Truthfully, I'm a little nervous about the reaction we might get when we arrive. There's a huge difference between being invited and actually showing up. Of course in my deranged fantasies, when I walk into the Popular Posse Party, I'm greeted with open arms (and an open mouth from Logan). *Something* tells me that's not going to happen here.

And that something is the buzz kill called reality.

"Do we knock or just go in?" I ask as I try the doorbell. I can hear the music blaring inside.

The door opens and it's Hannah. "Oh, hey, Lexi, come on in." She smiles politely at Cam and Benny.

"Welcome, *ladies*," Grant says as he looks over at Benny. "What can I get you *girls* to drink?"

Benny's face turns bright red as he looks at the door.

"Hey, Grant, have you met Benny? *He's* with us." I stare at Grant, almost daring him to say something else. Usually it's Cam who sticks up for us, but I'm not sitting down and staying silent anymore. I put my arm around Benny and start to walk through the house. Cam follows, completely shutting Grant out.

"I told you this was a bad idea," Benny whispers.

I have to admit that maybe he's right. It might've been unfair to bring Benny here. He gets attacked enough without me dragging him into a lion's den. I see him button up his plaid shirt so it covers his *Knight Rider* T-shirt.

"Let's just make a quick round so people can see us. Then we can leave," I promise him.

"Look, shelter." Cam points to a corner of the living room that's empty, and we decide to hold fort there. I take a look around and see that there are mostly the usual suspects here — Logan (*sigh* . . .), Alyssa, Taylor, Brooke — but not a whole lot of other "norms," if any at all.

Cam seems to be thinking the same thing. "Not as many people as I thought."

Fortunately, most people just nod at us as we sit down. So the three of us decide to carry on like it's a typical Saturday night, and we're in one of our houses goofing around, laughing.

"We want details of last night," I say to Benny. He was a nervous wreck all day yesterday leading up to his meeting with Chris. "Leave nothing out of your hot *date*."

Benny smiles shyly at us. I'm not used to seeing him so censored about his feelings. "It went well, but I don't really think it was a date."

"Stop it," I say. "You're being silly." But I can tell by the look on Benny's face that he's truly unclear on Chris's feelings about what yesterday was.

"I don't know. We had a great time — there wasn't a lull the entire night. He's even coming over next weekend to watch the first season of *The Facts of Life* with me. . . . It was a TV show."

"That's so great that you already have plans," I tell him. "He wants to see you again, so why don't you think it was a date?"

"I think he only sees me as a friend. We hugged at the end, which I guess is a good thing since I've never kissed a boy before, so I probably would do it wrong."

"I think kissing is kissing," I offer, although we both know I have no clue about that subject.

"Regardless, we can't assume it was a date just because we're both into boys. It's like, if a girl and a guy go out, you can assume it's a date, especially if the guy pays."

"Well, who paid?" I ask.

"He paid for coffee and I got dessert, but we're both guys, so . . ."

"First off," Cam begins to argue, "guys and girls can be friends without there being anything romantic involved."

"Yeah, *we're* friends." I counter.

Benny gives me an *are-you-being-serious?* look. "That's completely different. Do I really have to remind you that I'm not attracted to girls?"

"I don't know — you've been checking me out a lot this week," I tease. "But seriously, you're getting to know him. Who knows where it'll lead? And I have no doubt that the more he gets to know you, he'd be crazy not to fall for you. Just give it time."

Benny gives me a weak smile. "I guess. I'll try to not overanalyze everything and have fun."

"So, can we stop talking about boys for five seconds?" Cam asks. "Because I've finally made a decision."

My immediate thought is that she wants us to leave the party. And while we aren't really doing anything, I'm starting to feel comfortable here. Sure we're being ignored, but at least I can say that I was here, that I was invited. Although the only people I'd say this to are the ones sitting right next to me.

"Is this about school?" Benny asks.

Cam's parents have been pressuring her to graduate early even though she hasn't applied to any colleges yet. She's already taken all the hardest classes in school, she has enough credits to graduate, but there's something holding her back.

96

"Yeah . . . I . . ."

Both Benny and I find ourselves leaning in. Anytime either one of us has brought it up, she's changed the subject.

"Well —" She takes a deep breath. It's very disconcerting to see Cam self-conscious about something. "I'm not going to graduate this year. I'm staying."

A swell of relief spreads over me. As much as I want Cam to do what's best for her, I can't help but focus on the fact that her staying here would be best for me.

"Is that what you want?" I ask, guilty for even thinking about myself for a split second during this important decision for her.

She nods. "Yeah, well . . . I took a little too long and all the decent schools' deadlines have already passed. But I'm thinking that maybe me dragging my heels was really because I'm not ready to —"

"Oh my God." Benny's looking right past Cam and has a huge grin on his face. "Um, Lex, I think you have an admirer."

I turn around and see Taylor looking over at me. He raises his glass when our eyes meet.

"You should go over there," Benny prods.

"And do what?"

I turn to Cam for guidance, but she looks mad. I give her a *what-should-I-do?* look. She groans. "Oh, I don't know. *Talk* to him. Didn't you guys talk the other day when you waited on him?"

"Yeah, but there weren't a whole lot of sparks that flew during 'can I get you another size?' "

She lets out a little sigh. "You dragged us here. The least you could do is talk to somebody."

"Yeah!" Benny interjects. "And I thought the two of you looked so cute the other day. You have to go over there and single-handedly save this social black hole of an evening."

I'm about to get up, when I realize that I can't make this too easy on Benny.

"Fine, but only if you ask Chris out on a real date."

Benny's eyes are wide. "No way."

"Okay." I lean back on the couch and look in the opposite direction of Taylor.

Benny starts to shake his knee. "But he's right there, practically staring at you. You have to go over there."

I reach out and link my wrists as if my hands were tied. "You know my terms."

Benny looks back and forth between Taylor and me. "Okay, tomorrow night, I'll ask Chris to see a movie and *if* he says yes —"

"*When* he says yes." I correct him.

"Gah, fine! When he says yes, I'll say 'it's a date' and see what happens. That's as much as you'll get from me."

I give Benny a big smile as I get up and move across the room. I feel my pulse quicken with each step. For some reason, I think about what it must be like for Mac to approach the stage during the all-important interview portion of the pageant, with all of Mom's pointers going through her head. *Speak slowly and make eye contact.* I approach Taylor with my best confident smile. I feel like I'm applying for a job as a cool person.

Taylor leans against the wall, awaiting my arrival.

"Hey!" I say. "Nice shirt." *Start with a compliment.*

He looks down at one of the shirts I picked out for him and laughs. "Thanks. I've been getting lots of compliments on it. But, you know. I can't take credit for it."

"Behind every stylish guy is usually a smart girl." *Be funny, when appropriate.*

"*Especially* in this case." Taylor puts his hands in his jean pockets and leans back on his heels. "This party is kind of lame."

I nod. I haven't really been to a lot of parties, but it seems like all anybody is doing here is making out or getting drunk. Well, except for Benny, Cam, and me. We're just being ourselves. I hope *that* doesn't make us lame.

He leans in. "But at least you're here."

Okaaay.

He takes a swig of his cup. I don't have anything in my hand, so I just fold my arms and pretend that this isn't completely out of my realm.

"Hey, do you want to go grab a bite sometime? You know, I figure I owe you for all your help."

I'm thrown more than the time Mac was asked what her favorite part of being in a pageant was up on stage. It took her nearly ten seconds before she stammered out spending time with her mom. While the answer elicited *awwws* from the audience, ten seconds of silence on stage feels like an eternity.

He can't be, um, asking me on a date . . . or is he? I guess this is exactly what Benny was talking about. Is a guy and a girl going out together automatically a date? Is Taylor Riggins really asking me out on a date? No, he clearly thinks he owes me something. Better play dumb, which is *so* not hard to do under this circumstance.

"You don't need to do that. I was doing my job." I find myself nervously twisting my hair around my finger. So much for being composed.

He gives me a crooked smile. "I have to admit, you're really good at it. It was fun to watch you boss people around, even though the person you were ordering around was me."

There's an awkward pause. Like he's waiting for me to say something.

Does he think I'm not interested because I threw in the comment about my job? Because I *am* interested in going on a date. And that's what he's asking, right?

I guess I should try out some more of my flirting skills. Mental note: no crazy laughter or eyelash batting. Leave the intermediate stuff to the pros.

I touch his arm. "It was fun for me, too."

That's the best that I've got. *Seriously.*

He moves away from the wall and stands directly in front of me. "Okay, how about I take you out because I want to?"

Holy crap. Did that seriously just work?

Say something! "I guess that would be cool."

I guess that would be cool? Lexi, you finally get a guy to ask you out, and not just any guy, Taylor Riggins, and all you say is *I guess that would be cool?*

His face lights up. "Cool."

We both smile at each other. I'm not sure what to do next. He's the one who has experience in this stuff, not me.

"I guess I'll text you."

"Oh, okay." I give him a little smile before I turn back to Benny and Cam.

Best not to tempt fate any further.

"Let's go," I say as soon as I get back.

Benny and Cam jump out of their seats so quickly they've probably been waiting to hear me say that all evening.

The party has been lame, but I have a date.

Who knew playing dress-up could be so rewarding?

"I can't believe Taylor Riggins asked you out!" Benny shrieks once we get into the car. "I mean, not that I doubted a hottie would fall in love with you."

I can't respond because I'm still in shock.

Cam doesn't seem as pleased. "So you're cool that he only showed interest in you once you got all glam?"

"Yes!" Benny and I say in unison.

"So what's next?" Cam asks as she starts the car.

Benny practically shakes with excitement. "So let's see. Lexi goes on a date with *Taylor friggin' Riggins.*" Both Benny and I clap, the anticipation for my *first date* growing by the millisecond. "She makes him fall in love with her, which will happen in like, minute three of their date, they get married, move into a house with a white picket fence, and have a dozen kids. The end."

"I meant, your bet is over. You were supposed to glam up for the week," Cam reminds me. "What's he going to think come Monday?"

"Okay, okay!" Benny's practically jumping out of his seat. "If you glam it up on your date with Taylor, I'll —"

"Benny," I interrupt, "it's okay. I kind of like being this new person, and while I don't think I'll do the entire two-hour ritual every morning, I think I'm going to keep it up for a while. At least until my date."

My date. It sounds so foreign coming out of my mouth.

Benny's beaming. "And you don't want anything for it?"

"No, I think we both need to start doing things because we should be doing them," I say. "Except you still have to ask Chris on a date. But you should be willing to get to know him better to see if *you're* interested in him because it's important to put yourself out there. And I should do what makes me feel good, and if that's finally coming to terms with what happened all those years ago that caused me to think I couldn't be anything more than a runner-up . . ." I stop myself. Tonight's been an amazing evening; there's no point breaking down into tears. "I think that maybe we both need to believe in ourselves a little bit more."

Benny reaches over and gives me a hug. "You're right."

I'm right?

About time.

13.

Date Fright

I have a date.

I have a date with Taylor Riggins.

I, Lexi Anderson, have a date.

No matter how many times I say it, I still can't believe it.

For years I've been complaining about not being asked out on a date. I'll admit it bordered on annoying, although I'm sure Benny and Cam would laugh at *bordered*. But now I have a date.

And I'm totally freaking out.

I even have a new outfit — a black-and-white wrap dress with my knee-high boots. I have all my makeup lined up, but I keep staring at myself in the mirror.

Since the party, things have gotten even more surreal. Grant "you want me to take *Lexi* to Homecoming?" Christensen talks to me regularly now. Even Brooke doesn't look as disgusted when I'm in her presence. I keep getting compliments on my hair or clothes.

And I love every minute of it.

Rolling my hair and putting on my makeup has become easier for me. I don't have to think as much anymore, which can be a bad thing since it lets my mind wander.

I have no idea what to do on a date. Cam says for me to be myself, although being myself didn't land me the date in the first place.

But here's the messed-up part: I don't even know if I like Taylor. He's gorgeous, so I'd be stupid not to. But because I'm pathetic, all I keep thinking about is Logan. I was hoping that once I had a real date with a real boy my Logan delusions would end, or at least subside.

I push all the confusion out of my head while I put the finishing touches on my makeup. Since Taylor's coming in a few minutes, I go out in the living room, where Mackenzie is practicing her beauty walk for next weekend's pageant.

"My goodness, Lexi, come here." Mom pats the empty seat next to her. "I can't believe my baby girl has a date."

"Hey!" Mac sulks. "*I'm* your baby girl."

"Oh, honey, I know that. But I remember when Lexi was born like it was yesterday. So much has changed. . . ."

I look out the window, willing Taylor's car to pull up. I didn't want him to pick me up. I'm a little embarrassed about our house. We used to live in a nice little three-bedroom, two-story house with a two-car garage. Dad's child support didn't fully cover the mortgage, so because of the rising costs of the pageants we had to move into this glorified double-wide.

Mac looks me up and down. She hasn't been very supportive of my recent makeover. She got upset at the pageant this past weekend when I got a bunch of compliments on my outfit. I hate to say it, but I sometimes think that she feels like she's the only person in the entire universe who deserves to be praised for her beauty. And unfortunately, I know *exactly* where she got that idea.

Mac folds her arms. "Where are you getting the money for all your new clothes?"

"I have a *job* at a *clothing* store, remember?" I don't feel the need to defend my spending habits to her.

Mac turns to Mom. "Why does *she* get new clothes when *I* have to wear an old gown this weekend?"

"Because I have a JOB."

Another side effect from this newfound confidence is that I'm starting to confront the fact that I'm not really appreciated that much in my family. It seems like the only time Mom and Mac want anything to do with me is when they need something from me. And when Mac gets a crown or a title, I'm not even thanked. I know that she's the one up on stage, but I'm the one up early running around catering to their every demand. If Mac wants sour-cream-and-onion potato chips, I have to find them. If Mom needs another one of her frozen coffee drinks, it's me who gets it. If Mac starts to kick the makeup person when she doesn't want fake eyelashes applied, I'm the one who has to hold her feet.

But before I can start an argument, Taylor pulls up in his car. Like a knight riding in on a white horse.

"He's here. I'll see you later." I start to walk out.

"Now wait just a second, I want to meet this guy." Mom gets up.

"Please, Mom, maybe another time?" I realize that I sound desperate. This evening's stressful enough without having to worry about being embarrassed by my family.

Mom glances at Mackenzie, who's currently wearing one of her crowns and sashes and is waving her hand around, smiling. "Okay, but next time, I expect to meet him."

"Of course, thanks!" I rush outside and see Taylor approaching the house.

He smiles at me. "Hey, I was planning on knocking. It's the gentlemanly thing to do."

"That's sweet of you, but there's pageant craziness going on in there."

Taylor laughs and does a little wave. I turn around to find both Mackenzie and my mom staring out the window.

So much for not being embarrassed.

"Shall we . . ." I start walking toward the car.

"You look great."

"Thanks!" That will never, and I mean *never*, get old.

* * *

When I thought about being on a date, I never thought about the details. My mind would focus on specific moments, like when Logan would pick me up at my house. Of course, in my dreams it was always a fabulous house, not the dump I currently inhabit. He'd bring me flowers. He'd stare in my eyes. We'd walk along some beach holding hands, with the warm waves gently brushing against our feet. (Don't ask me where we found an ocean in Dallas.) We'd make out, there'd be fireworks, we'd get married and live happily ever after.

So I'm not *entirely* surprised that a regular, or I guess I should say *real*, first date isn't anything like what I've dreamed of. But I didn't realize that I would have so many things to consider, beyond what I was going to wear.

Taylor opens up the passenger-side door for me, which I know is chivalrous and all, but I'm not expecting it, so I nearly fall over on the grass when I abruptly stop to let him open it for me. So am I supposed to wait in the car after we park for him to open the door for me? Is that what girls do? It makes me feel like he's my chauffeur if I just sit there and wait for him to go around and open up the door. I don't want to seem like a snob, or lazy, but what if he wants to open it for me?

And where do I put my hands? I've been a passenger in a car thousands of times before. But as I sit here next to Taylor, who's telling me some story about football that I'm pretending to be interested in, I'm hyperaware of his proximity to me. I've currently got my hands resting in my lap like I'm a lady in the 1920s waiting for her gentleman caller to show up.

And what happens when the bill arrives? I know I should offer to pay, even though if he pays that means it's a date. And if he lets me split the bill, does that mean he isn't having a good time? Or that this is just a friend thing? I guess I should be careful not to order anything too expensive. Maybe just a side salad or something. And a water. Oh God, I think that's probably what Brooke eats on dates.

And if he does pay, then should I pay for the movie? I should offer that. Shouldn't I? I don't even know what I'll do with my hands during the movie. And I think I'll have a heart attack if I even start entertaining thoughts about the end of the evening and a possible kiss.

And I guess the most important question of all: Is this even a real date? I mean, he asked me. But not really *me*, like Normal Lexi. He asked the primped-out version of me. So I don't know if I can really consider this a real date. It's been built on false pretenses.

But then why am I so nervous?

"Ready?" Taylor shuts off the ignition and I realize that we're at the mall.

I try to give him a confident smile. "Yes!" And I open the passenger door and get out.

That's one less thing I have to worry about.

Of course, the second I get home, I call Benny.

He picks up the phone before I even hear a ring. "So?"

"I love how me having a date is such a momentous occasion that you're literally waiting by your phone."

"Um, a date with *Taylor Riggins*. Spill it. Now."

I hesitate for a few seconds.

"Are you going to make me beg?"

"It went well. . . ."

"Well?"

"Yeah, we went to Leo's for dinner, then saw that new Wesley Pike movie. It was fun. . . . I just don't know. I'm not sure if he's really into me."

I hear Benny sigh. "Do I need to come over there and smack you? This is basically the same thing I said to you about Chris, and do I need to remind you how foolish you thought I was being? He asked you on a *date* — what part of *he's interested in you* do you fail to understand?"

"No, I know. It's only . . ." I flicker back to just a moment ago. "At the end of the date, I was sort of expecting him to kiss me or try something. And he just hugged me good-bye and said that it was fun and we should do it again soon."

My cheeks become hot as I think of me standing there outside our front door like an idiot. Thinking he was going to kiss me, that I was going to have my first real kiss. But then . . . nothing.

Every time I envisioned what it would be like, it started out the way we were just a few moments ago. Logan walks me to my front door, he tells me what an amazing time he had (which Taylor did), then he tucks a stray piece of hair behind my ear, but he doesn't pull his hand away.

Instead he cups my face, and leans in and gives me the single greatest kiss in the history of first dates.

I mean, is that so much to ask?

"Wait a second." Benny snaps me back to reality. "So because he didn't shove his tongue down your throat, you're convinced that he's not into you? Has the thought ever crossed your mind that he's being a gentleman?"

"I don't know how these things work. Cam's always talking about guys trying to put the moves on her any chance they get. I guess I was expecting the same thing. I'm new to this; I'm only going off of what she says happens —"

I hear a text come through and lift up my phone to see it.

"Hello?" Benny shouts.

"Sorry, I'm here. I got a text from Taylor."

"AND?"

"It says 'Had a great time, let's do it again soon.'"

Benny groans. "See! I told you."

"You're right." I hesitate for a moment. "Benny, I haven't really thanked you."

"Nor I you," he reminds me. "But this is what friends do. We remind each other how awesome we are."

I laugh. "Benny, can you believe we both may have boyfriends?"

"Crap," he says — not the response I thought I'd get. "Does this mean the world's going to end?"

14.

The Road to Popularity Is Paved with Questionable Intentions

I t's pretty clear that I don't know how to act on a date. But how to act at school after the first date is especially agonizing. Am I supposed to act different around Taylor? Has anybody written *The Dating Guide for Clueless Teenage Girls* yet? I *need* that book.

Fortunately for me, I do know someone who can clarify this mystery. And she's headed straight toward me. Unfortunately, Cam doesn't look too happy. The minute she gets to me, she says, "Have you seen Brooke's pictures from Grant's party on her profile?"

Okay, if there isn't even a hello from Cam, this can't be good.

"That would require me to be friends with Brooke. Why?"

Cam looks around. I follow her gaze and realize that some people are staring at me. A few are even whispering.

"She took some photos of us, mostly you, and made some comments."

My stomach drops. "What kind of comments?"

"When you click on your face, instead of saying your name it said things like 'desperate,' 'wannabe,' 'troll' — stupid things like that."

"Oh." I can't get anything else out. I can't think of anything else to say. I guess I shouldn't be surprised about what she did; it's pretty typical of her. But even if I was anticipating something like this, it still doesn't make it any easier to stomach.

Cam gives me a tight smile. "Don't let it get you down. She's just jealous. Ignore her and she's bound to go away."

I'm guessing that ignoring Brooke will be easier said than done, but I try to push those words out of my mind. Is that how she really sees me? Does everybody else see me that way?

Cam gives me a hug before she heads to class. I do my best to shake the negative thoughts from my head and not let it get to me. I see Benny approach with a sympathetic frown on his face.

News sure gets around fast.

"It's okay," I say before he can get a word in. The last thing I need is for one more person to feel sorry for me. I wrap my arm around Benny's. "Let's get to class."

We round the corner to English when we see Brooke approaching me with a smile on her face.

Benny leans in. "Do you want me to . . ."

"It's okay."

Actually, it *isn't* okay. But what can I really do about it? Saying something would definitely make it worse.

"Hey, Lexi," she says sweetly as she blocks Benny and me from proceeding farther down the hallway, which is quite amazing since she's so tiny, but her intimidation factor is through the roof. "We *need* to hang out more. I'd *love* to go shopping with you sometime. You have such *ah*-mazing taste in clothing. I'll text you!" And without another word, she walks past us.

Benny breaks the stunned silence between us. "What was that?"

"I have no idea." Does she think that I wouldn't hear about what she did? Or does she think that she can break me so easily? Why would she even want to hang out with a "wannabe" and a "troll"? And does she even know what a troll is? I'm a few inches taller than her, so what, exactly, would that make her?

Benny clicks his teeth in disgust. "You're not going, are you?"

"What? Going where?"

"Shopping. With Brooke."

I give a nondescript shrug of my shoulders. Part of me has no desire to be around her. Ever. But another part of me wants to see what game she's playing.

And okay, there's another part of me, a very teeny, tiny part, that wants her acceptance.

If you would've told me a month ago that I'd be invited to a party at Grant's and go on a date with Taylor, I would've said that you were living in a fantasy world. But what I'm doing right here, right now? Well, I would've put myself in a loony bin at the mere thought of it even two days ago. Yet here I am.

Brooke rummages through the rack at an upscale department store in the mall. I visit this place every once in a while to see what they have out, but I could never afford anything here.

"So . . ." Brooke addresses me without taking her eyes off of a long black tank dress she has in her hands. "How are things with Taylor?"

Is that why she asked to do something with me? To find out about my, ah, relationship with Taylor? *Oh my goodness, am I in a relationship?* I pick up a jacket near me and pretend to study the zipper, delaying a response. I don't know what to say. I know anything I tell Brooke will be around the school in 2.4 seconds.

"Good. I'm seeing him tomorrow night."

A ringing sound comes from Brooke's very expensive red leather satchel.

"Ugh, it's Hannah," Brooke says as she silences her phone. "Isn't she *so* needy?" she asks expectantly.

I don't respond. Hannah's always been nice enough to me. I thought she and Brooke were BFFs, but I guess with Brooke it's BFFN (Best Friends For Now).

It's funny, because in a way, Brooke reminds me of a few of the pageant girls. She clearly abides by one of their most sacred pageant rules: *If you don't have anything nice to say, wait until her back is turned.*

Brooke heads into the dressing room without another word, probably unsatisfied with my lack of trash talking.

I continue to look around the store, wondering why I even agreed to this. I guess it's more out of curiosity than anything else. But I can completely understand that Benny and Cam aren't too pleased that I'd go, as Cam put it, "shopping with the enemy." After I told her I was going today, she slammed her head down on the lunch table so loudly that half the cafeteria turned around. She had a red blotch on her forehead for the remainder of the day. Then she told me that she'd disown me if I turned into a Beauty Bot and started eating lunch at the Popular Posse table. I had to pinkie swear that I would never do such a horrific thing.

"Are you coming or not?" I hear Brooke call out from the dressing room.

I walk in and see her in front of a three-way mirror examining herself from every angle.

"What do you think?"

I've been asked this question hundreds of times at work. Generally people ask it when they aren't positive they like something or have a concern. But with Brooke, I think she only wants positive reinforcement. Which is hard in this instance, because while the dress looks nice on her, it gaps where her armpits are, since she's so tiny but has a big chest for her frame. It really doesn't look good, but I'm terrified of saying anything.

"Well . . ." I try to think of what I should say, but I don't want to lie. I hate being manipulated and don't feel comfortable doing it to someone, even if that someone is Queen Manipulator. Maybe she would even appreciate someone telling her the truth for once. "I think . . . that maybe it fits a little weird around the arms."

Brooke lifts her arms and can see that her purple lace bra is showing with the gap in the dress.

"It's more a flaw with the design of the dress," I add.

She goes into the dressing room with a slam of the door.

Mental note for the future: *Do NOT tell the truth. Just say she looks great.*

I hear my stomach growl. "Hey, Brooke," I call out to her. "I'm getting hungry, do you want to grab something to eat?"

"No."

I reach in my purse and grab a cherry pie Lärabar. I'm halfway through eating it when she opens up her dressing room door and stares at me.

"Wow. You eat *a lot*."

I look down at my super-healthy snack. "Um, you're supposed to eat every few hours. Do you want one?"

I dig through my purse.

"No." She scrunches up her nose at me.

"Are you sure? It's good. They're gluten free." I stop myself from giving Brooke the same food lecture I give my mom. The difference between the two is that all my mom eats is junk, while I'm pretty sure Brooke doesn't eat at all. I know it's not fair of me to make assumptions about Brooke, because Cam's super skinny and eats more than me and Benny combined. But I've never seen Brooke eat anything more than a few bites of food.

Brooke takes a piece of gum out of her bag. "I'm sure." She gives me the death stare as she puts the stick in her mouth.

I give up, and honestly I could care less about what Brooke thinks.

But then, if I don't care, what am I doing here?

"Well, well . . ." Mark knocks on the employee break room door at the end of my shift the following day. He gives me a little smirk. "Your *guest* is here. It all starts making sense."

I finish changing into my cute date shoes and ignore his comment. I give myself a quick once-over in the mirror and grab my purse.

Mark has the door blocked. "I'm trying to figure out if he bought all those clothes weeks ago because he liked you, or if you're dating him as a thanks for the commission. Either way, the dedication to your job has not gone unnoticed."

I move his arm away and go into the store to see Taylor browsing.

"Hey," I say to get his attention.

"Hi." He smiles at me and gives me a quick hug.

"Ahem." Mark clears his voice loudly.

I can't believe he's going to make me introduce him like he's my parent. Well, sometimes Mark acts more like a father figure to me than my *actual* father.

"Mark, this is Taylor; Taylor, this is my boss, Mark."

They shake hands.

"So where are you two off to?" Mark asks.

"Just going to grab a bite at The Court." I give him a smile that says *Don't push it any further.*

Mark starts to rub his chin, like he's deep in thought. "I see. And how late will you be this evening?"

"Don't wait up." I grab Taylor's arm and head out to the mall. "Sorry about that. I'd like to say that he's a little overprotective, but basically he just likes to humiliate me."

"Oh good." Taylor seems flustered. "Not good that he humiliates you, I got worried that I'd have yet another guy who would threaten me if anything happens to you."

Taylor can tell from my reaction that I have no idea what he's talking about.

He leans in close to me. "Your friend Benny came up to me today. He said that he hoped I had fun tonight, but not too much fun."

"Oh my God, no he didn't. You're lying!"

He holds up his arms. "I kid you not. He's a big guy, I have to admit, it freaked me out a bit. I didn't realize he could be so intimidating. We've got to get him on the football team."

I can't believe Benny would do that. It makes me love him even more. Although the chances of Benny joining the football team are as likely as me becoming BFFN with Brooke.

"Anyway, Josh told me that new mini-golf place is pretty cool. You want to try it out on Saturday?"

We haven't even finished our second date and he's already asking me on a third? The excitement I feel dies quickly as I realize what's this Saturday.

"I can't on Saturday. I have to go help out at my sister's pageant." Not to mention that I was supposed to see my father.

Taylor studies my face. "That must be hard to have to devote so much time to your little sister."

I'm almost speechless. I'm used to dropping everything for the pageants, but truthfully, it *can* be a burden. And never did I think someone like Taylor would notice.

"It can be pretty frustrating. . . ." I allow myself to speak the truth for once. But I can't really elaborate, out of fear of what would come out of my mouth.

My phone comes to life. I glance at the screen and see it's Mom.

"Do you need to . . ." Taylor motions toward my phone.

"Um, it's my mom, I should probably . . ."

I pick up the phone and move to the corner of the food court. I hate when people talk on their phones in public, especially in the mall. I can't even begin to describe some of the horribly personal conversations I've had to listen to while at work. I usually try to get as far away from the people as possible, but there are only so many places I can hide on the floor. Just last week a woman came in and started breaking up with her boyfriend on the phone, all while searching the rack for her size.

"Thank goodness you picked up." Mom sounds out of breath.

"Hello to you, too."

"I need you to take your sister to her dance class."

Of course she needs me to do something.

"When?" I don't even bother to hide the annoyance in my voice.

"The class starts in fifteen so you need to get over here ASAP."

"But I'm with Taylor and we —"

"Not now, Lexi." She cuts me off. "I got called into work to cover some-body who's out sick, and we could really use the extra money. Come and pick your sister up and take her. It really isn't a big deal. See you soon."

And she hangs up. Because she knows I'll come. Because she really couldn't care less what I have going on, even if it's a date with a boy.

Because what I want never seems to matter, does it?

"Is everything okay?" Taylor looks at me with concern.

"Oh, um, yes . . . Well, no. I have to go and take my sister to dance practice."

"Do you want me to come with you?" he offers.

God no. The last thing I want is to have to drag anybody else onto Planet Mackenzie.

"It's okay, I should go. Sorry, um . . ."

Taylor smiles and rubs my back. "That sucks. Well, I guess I'll see you later."

He's being so nice. I wonder if I'm part of some plan for him. Like charity work or something. There has to be a reasonable explanation for all of this. There's no way a makeover can have this kind of power over any guy. No matter what *Teen Vogue* says.

I excuse myself and head to my car. To do the bidding of a seven-year-old diva.

It seems like I can have whatever plan I want, but somehow, some-way, the pageants always have to come first. No matter what.

15.

I'm So Not Ready for My Close-up

I don't know why I'm shocked that Mackenzie's having a tantrum. But instead of being tired or upset about her hair or outfit, she's freaking out over *my* outfit.

"Then make her take it off." Mac stamps her foot on the floor.

"Take what off, sweetie?" Mom asks.

"All of it — her makeup, that outfit. Why isn't she wearing her Team Mackenzie shirt? Why is she wearing *that*?"

Mackenzie points to the outfit I wore for my first date with Taylor. It isn't anything super special, although I did get some compliments on my way in from the regular pageant goers who until today didn't realize I was a girl or had a figure.

Honestly, I can't believe Mom isn't making me wear the T-shirt to the *Texas Beauty Tykes* interview. She's proudly wearing hers.

"Sweetie," Mom says in the high cooing voice she reserves for Mackenzie's worst days, "we've got to go downstairs and meet with the producers. Don't you want to be on TV?"

Mac scrunches up her face. "Not if *she's* going to be there." She points at me dramatically.

Yes, me. The girl who should be spending the weekend with her father. The one who has to pull a double shift tomorrow at work to make up for bailing on yet another Saturday to attend a pageant. Me, who could be playing mini golf with Taylor right at this very moment.

What's odd is that Mac has never minded me being at the pageant as long as I did what I was told and wore the Team Mackenzie T-shirt. But the times, they clearly are a-changing.

"They want to meet the whole family," Mom says, ignoring the fact that we're down one father figure.

"Honestly, Mackenzie." I figure someone's got to try to talk some sense into her. "You yourself said that I'm ugly, so I don't know why it bothers you so much that I'm just trying to be like my *gorgeous* baby sister." I smile sweetly at her.

"You're doing this to make fun of me and everything about pageants."

Wow. I've been underestimating Mackenzie all this time. She knows way more than she lets on.

"Honey" — Mom glances at her watch — "if you want to be on TV, we've got to go now. Lexi isn't going to say anything to the producers." She turns to me and gives me a warning look. "Are you, Lexi?"

"Of course not."

And I mean it. I plan on playing the role of the saintly mute. And if, Lord help us, we get accepted, I'll overbook myself at work and stay over at Benny's. There's no way I want to be on television. Sure, someday I want my designs to be featured during Fashion Week or on the red carpet. However, I don't want my fifteen minutes (more like fifteen seconds) to be on *Texas Beauty Tykes*.

Mackenzie gets up and makes a big production out of leaving. As if she's doing us a favor. Like the draw of the spotlight isn't enough to motivate her to do anything.

We head downstairs to the conference room where the producers are meeting with potential targets — I mean *participants*. There are nearly twenty girls in line, from ages two to ten. Nervous mothers pace the hallway.

We see Lauren come out of the room.

"Miss Lauren!" Mackenzie runs over and gives her a hug.

"Well, hey, sweetie. Great to see you. The producers were asking me about you."

"They were?" Mom puts her hand to her heart for extra effect.

"Yes, ma'am." Lauren gives Mom an encouraging pat on her back. "They know I've worked on a lot of the girls here so they asked for my thoughts. And of course, I said nothing but glowing things about our Miss Mackenzie."

Lauren's face lights up when she gets a look at me. "Why, Lexi! Look at you, gorgeous!"

I give her a giant hug. "All thanks to you."

She waves me off. "Just helping to highlight what God gave you."

I lean in so Mom and Mac can't hear. "Thanks. I cut out some looks in a few magazines I was hoping maybe you could help me with."

"Of course! Find me after the interview."

"Really? Thanks so much!" I clap my hands really fast and throw my head back in laughter — giddy, squealy, very un-Lexi schoolgirl laughter. I've noticed a few of the people waiting for the producers are looking at me.

Better rein it in.

Lauren wishes us luck as Mom heads into the room. The producers asked to speak with the parents first, so Mac and I wait for her outside.

"Why are you doing this to me?" Mackenzie's voice is strained. I look over and see her face getting really red.

"Doing what?"

She looks at me with her big eyes. "Why are you walking around like you're auditioning for some makeover show? And why are you trying to create a scene at the pageant? This is supposed to be about me."

"It's *always* about you, Mackenzie."

"No, it's not."

126

"Oh, okay." I don't say anything else. As much as I don't want to do this show, I don't want to get Mac upset before she has to go in.

"All you do is spend time with your friends," she says in a small voice.

Yeah, like I'm doing right now. My annoyance is growing by the second. It's amazing that I'm allowed to have any time away from her kingdom.

Her voice is nearly inaudible. "At least Dad likes you."

"What?" I look at Mackenzie and see she's near tears. I check around to make sure nobody can see her. "Mac, you know that's not true. Dad loves you. We were supposed to be with him today. Remember? And he was so sad to not see you."

"No, he was sad he couldn't be with *you*. He wanted *you* to still come."

"He did?"

How does she know that?

"I listened in on the phone conversation. He told Mom that I should stop doing pageants and they're a waste of time."

I bite my tongue. I once suggested we cut back on going to pageants because they were costing too much money and Mom didn't talk to me for a week. I know better now.

She sniffles. "And he didn't even ask to speak to me. He only wanted to talk to you."

"Mac, he's known me longer than you. I guess we have more stuff to say to each other. And you're usually so busy doing pageants so he doesn't get to see you as much as he sees me. But, I . . ." I don't really

127

know what to say. I can't say she brings it upon herself because she's only seven years old.

"What's wrong?" We both look up to see Mom looking concerned. "What's the matter?"

"Nothing," Mac says quietly.

Mom turns to me. "What did you do?"

"I . . ."

Okay, *seriously*? Why is this my fault? And why does she automatically assume that I did something?

I'm really getting sick of this. And I don't know why it has taken this long for me to finally see how ridiculous this all is. Not the pageants — I've known that forever. But the way I'm treated by my own family.

I have got to find a way to get out of coming to these things for good.

"Let's go." Mackenzie gets up and heads to the room.

Mom glares at me. "What on earth —"

I don't let her finish. "Has it ever crossed your mind that *I* didn't do anything? That maybe Mac is upset about something other than pageants?"

"For heaven's sake, Lexi, this is not the time to start trouble. Not before Mackenzie has an interview with television producers." She looks at me with such disgust. "And on second thought, don't come in. You've already done enough."

Mom turns on her heel and chases after Mac.

I don't know how much more of this I can take.

*

"Is this seat taken?" An older gentleman, obviously a pageant dad, gestures toward the seat next to me.

"All yours." I give him a weak smile.

"I couldn't help but notice your little argument. Was that your mother?"

I'm taken aback. I've seen plenty of families melt down at these pageants. You usually just keep your head down and try not to get hit by any flying objects.

"Oh, yeah, it's nothing. Just stress," I lie.

"Are you auditioning?"

"Oh, no." I can't help but laugh. "My sister's in there now. I think I'm a little too old to be considered a tyke."

He gives me a warm smile. "Do you watch the show?"

"*Texas Beauty Tykes*? I don't really need to watch it — I *live* that show. Is your daughter auditioning?"

He shakes his head. "No, simply observing. No matter how many pageants I go to, I can't get used to all the silliness."

I extend my hand. "Hello, fellow sane person. Pleased to meet a normal in the loony bin."

He laughs, then takes my hand. "Tom."

"Lexi."

"So, Lexi, I take it that you're not a fan of pageants, then?" He takes off his wire-rimmed glasses and starts polishing them with his button-down checkered shirt.

I hesitate. Generally when I'm asked about my opinion of pageants, I give a canned response: *"They're wonderful, they help build self-esteem, my beloved baby sister just loves them. . . ."*

But I'm not in the best mood right now to hold back and pretend that everything's okay. Because I'm tired of it all. I'm tired of how much pageants take away from me, from my family. I'm tired of lying, or not being able to express my feelings. Of having to stay silent.

I've been asked my opinion, and Uncensored Lexi is going to give it.

"Not really. It's just . . . they cost so much money, and there's no way you're ever going to earn it back. Even if you win every single Ultimate Grand Supreme title, there's no way to come out ahead. Every pageant costs us at least a thousand dollars, money we don't have. And all I keep hearing is that it helps build self-esteem, but in my opinion, it builds brats. My little sister is the worst. Everything in our house revolves around her. And all Mom does is smile and say she has a 'big personality' or is 'spirited,' which at the end of the day means she's a spoiled brat.

"Sorry, once you get me started . . ." I look around, making sure Mom hasn't heard my tirade. I feel bad calling Mac a brat, but let's face it, she can be one. And Mom does nothing to discipline her, especially on Pageant Day.

Tom smiles at me. "Oh no, I agree with what you're saying. Go on."

I realize how much better I feel finally letting it all out. I wonder if this guy would be okay with me lying down on a couch. This is totally therapy for me.

"I mean, do you really have to spend over a grand just so someone can come home with a crown to make her feel special? Like, what does it say about society that the only way you can feel good about yourself is if you put on a ton of —"

I stop myself even though Tom's nodding in agreement with me. I'm such a hypocrite, complaining about how shallow it is to praise someone for their looks, even though I spent over an hour this morning primping to be behind-the-scenes. I'm pretending that I don't get excited every day to be complimented on my new look, that putting on the pretty hasn't made *me* more confident.

Maybe Mac and I aren't that different after all.

"Sorry." A feeling of guilt starts to spread over me. I shouldn't talk so openly about my disgust for pageants in the middle of a pageant. These moms can be fierce.

Tom laughs. "Oh no, please continue. . . ."

I'm starting to wonder what this guy's deal is. Why is he getting so much joy out of my ragging on pageants? Worse still, what if he's *friends* with my mom?

I turn the attention on him. "What age division is your daughter?"

He shakes his head. "Oh, I'm not here with a contestant. I'm one of the producers of the show."

Holy butt glue.

Just then Mom and Mackenzie exit the interview room. Mac looks ecstatic, while Mom seems defeated.

Tom sees them coming as well.

"Well, I guess I should let you go. Great talking with you, Lexi. Really, great." He hands me his business card. Thomas Woodhouse, Associate Producer, *Texas Beauty Tykes.*

Yeah, great.

Mom will end my life if she finds out that I ruined Mackenzie's chances at reality TV infamy.

I used to spend the majority of pageants watching with my eyeballs rolled up into my skull, but today I decide on a different approach. I knew there were some correlations between pageants and being in high school, but once I pay attention, it's a little shocking.

Generally speaking, tight, sparkly outfits get the most positive response from the crowd/The Chosen Ones. Confident poses elicit the most head nodding from the judges/jocks. Lighter-haired girls are the biggest winners (a.k.a. Alyssa, but we already knew that).

I start writing all this down to tell Benny later.

"Are you taking *notes?*" Logan gestures toward the notebook in my hand.

"Oh, yeah." Although I don't think Logan would appreciate my theories. "Just a little . . . experiment."

He studies my face for a moment. I do my best to not look away.

"It seems like you've been doing a lot of, ah, experiments lately."

I can't help but smile. "For example?"

It doesn't take a rocket scientist to figure out that something's going on with me; I'm curious to see what Logan's theory is. I've heard the current rumor around school is that I want to try out for cheerleading next year.

As if.

"I don't know." He shrugs his shoulders, his magnificent broad shoulders. . . . "You seem a little different."

"So is that a good or a bad thing?" I can't believe I'm being so blunt with him. Never did I think I'd have the confidence to pretty much ask Logan if he thinks I'm hot. I mean, that's basically what's going on here, right?

"No, it's all fine." He looks straight ahead, refusing to make eye contact with me. "It seems to have come out of nowhere. Like, I wasn't aware that you had a thing for Taylor, that's all."

Hmmm, jealous much?

I shrug. "I wasn't aware that I needed to give you my diary to read."

He laughs. "I don't mean it like that. It's only . . . I didn't realize that you had so many surprises up your sleeve." He finally meets my eyes. And instead of doing what I usually do, which is melt into a pile of boy-crazy blubber, I decide to do something that I've never done before.

I'm going to flirt with Logan Reeves.

I give him a mischievous smirk and raise my left eyebrow. "Oh, Logan, you have no idea of all the surprises I have."

And I can't help but think that maybe, just maybe, he'll flirt right back.

"Yeah, well." He crosses his arms and leans back in his chair. "Taylor's a good guy, one of my best friends. We should go on a double date sometime."

On second thought . . .

I nod in reply. I guess that could be fun. I've never been that great watching Logan and Alyssa go all couply in front of me, but if I was with Taylor . . . I make a mental note to call him later. Between his practices, my work, me being Mac's personal chauffeur, and this pageant, we haven't been able to have a third date. But we've been talking every day. He's even sent me a few texts to see how I'm holding up with all the pageant craziness.

Logan and I sit in silence during the crowning. Mackenzie technically got first in her age group (although two girls in her division "pulled out," which means they got a bigger overall title), so it'll be a pleasant car ride home.

Logan gives me a little nod good-bye before he walks over to kiss Alyssa.

I'll just remove that knife sticking through my heart, thank you very much.

I go over to Mac and Mom, and to my horror see *Texas Beauty Tykes* Tom approach us. I shut my eyes and will him to go speak to someone else, to not mention the things I said to him.

I open my eyes and see him in front of Mom. "Excuse me, Ms. Anderson? I'm with the production team, and we'd love to have a word with you and your family."

Mom's eyes widen. "Of course. Come on, Mackenzie."

Tom gestures toward me. "We'd like Lexi as well."

"Oh!" Mom looks between the producer and me, although I refuse to make eye contact with either of them. Instead I'm pretending like I'm really interested in the banners on stage. "Of course."

I feel Mom's hand on my arm as we head into the room next door where they were doing the interviews. I won't look at her, or acknowledge that I know exactly why Tom knows my name.

Tom gestures to the three chairs that are lined up for us. "Please have a seat."

The three of us sit down in front of Tom and a few other people. Introductions are made. Mom and Mackenzie are smiling and being their perfect pageant selves. I feel like I'm about to be interrogated.

Tom smiles. "We have some great news." *I guess that would depend on who you're talking to.* "We'd like to talk about featuring your family in an upcoming episode."

Mom puts her hand up to her heart. "Oh my goodness, this is just the best news *ever*. Isn't it Mackenzie?"

Mackenzie gives them her pageant smile.

I try not to look like a deer caught in headlights.

This can't be happening.

He continues, "We think you have a great family story, and we especially like the dynamic between the two sisters. We aren't used to seeing such a big gap in the age of siblings, and well, to be honest, their opinions on pageants."

Wow, these lightbulbs are bright. I wonder how many there are in this room? Maybe if I stare at them long enough I'll go blind and have to leave to go to the hospital. Yes, an injury would be really great right now. Because a self-inflicted wound will be a lot better than the damage that'll be done if Mom finds out that I talked to any of the *Tykes* people.

Oh, who am I kidding, I *went off* on him.

Mom says in her best sugary-sweet, *everything-is-perfect-in-my-family* voice, "Lexi loves helping her little sister, don't you, Lex?"

Mom's giving me one of those *don't-you-dare-mess-this-up* looks.

I know exactly what these producers are looking for. And I'm going to make sure that they get the exact *opposite* of that.

I turn to them and put on a nice, big pageant smile. (I'm pretty sure I look insane.) "Oh yes, I think what the pageants have done for my darling baby sister is priceless. There's such a sense of community within these young ladies. And they're learning such important life skills that they'll be able to carry with them throughout their lives."

Even without turning, I can tell that both Mom and Mac are about to fall over from shock.

I keep smiling at the producers as they start whispering among themselves.

"I'm sorry, Lexi," one of the other producers says to me, "we were under the impression that you hated pageants and thought they were a waste of money."

I feign being stunned. "Goodness gracious, I don't know what on earth would ever give you such an impression. My word!" I don't know why I suddenly find the need to talk as if I'm a character straight out of *Gone with the Wind*.

Tom's face turns red. "How about your conversation with me?"

"When did you speak to him?" Mom's pageant face has been erased and her *I'm-going-to-kill-you-Lexi* face has returned.

"When you were in here. Lexi was extremely vocal about her disgust for the pageant world."

How odd that he didn't choose to use the word *entrapment* to describe our encounter.

Although is this really considered news to Mom? I know I've made comments, but has she really ignored them all? Does my opinion really matter that little to her?

In order to stop a major scene, which is what they're looking for, I stand up.

I feel my body tremble, but I force myself to look at each of the producers in the eye. I know I get annoyed about pageants and Princess Mackenzie, but at the end of the day, she's my sister. I will protect her as best I can.

Nobody puts baby sis in a corner.

I take a deep breath. "I'm aware of what I said outside. Although, I *wasn't* aware that I was speaking to a producer and that *is* my fault. But I do need to make something clear. If you come into our house, you're only going to encounter Encouraging and Supportive Lexi, the *bestest* big sister in the whole wide world. I will not allow you to humiliate my family or take advantage of my baby sister, who, despite my feelings about pageants, I love very much. So if you're looking for some extreme fighting among siblings, you aren't going to get it here."

I walk out of the room. Even with my back turned, I can feel every eyeball on me, including a very angry pair.

I try to compose myself for a few minutes before Mom and Mac come back out. I know I've ruined this for Mackenzie. But I've seen that show, I've seen how most of the contestants look like brats and are humiliated after the episode airs. Yes, I called Mackenzie a brat, and at times she can be, but I don't want her to be made fun of.

I remember being seven. I loved that age. Being seven's awesome. You don't have that much responsibility or homework. And it's illegal to work, so you get to play a lot. Being seven rocks. Or it should rock.

Mom and Mac exit the room. Mom walks over to me and grabs my arm, hard.

"They don't want us now. Are you happy? How could you do this to your sister?"

I refuse to back down. Enough is enough. "How could *you* do this to *your* daughter, *Mom*?"

She leads me over to a corner so we're away from a large group of gossipy pageant moms, all waiting to make one last plea for their children to be featured on the show. "What are you even talking about? Do you have any idea what a big deal this would've been for your sister?"

"Big deal for what? Three of the girls here today have been featured on that show. All it does is shed light on money problems, family tension . . . I've never seen one person come out of that show who made me think, *Well, they're not* totally *made of pure evil.*"

"You're just jealous of your sister. That's obviously why you've been prancing around like a —" Mom closes her mouth quickly.

I get in her face. We're only inches away from each other. "Like a what? Say it. Because I'm wearing half the makeup you put on your seven-year-old daughter to strut around on stage in a bikini in front of strangers. Yeah, so let's start judging the sixteen-year-old for *looking her age*. Or are you upset that I'm walking proof that you're wrong? Because I'm not ugly."

Mom's jaw drops. "I never said —"

"Yes, you did." I try to resist the memory that starts flooding back to me.

"You're just being silly." She waves me away like she doesn't have a clue what I'm talking about.

It kills me that she doesn't even remember what happened. That one moment, one that was so inconsequential for her, molded the person that I am today.

It comes back to me like it was just yesterday, even though it was five years ago; Mac was about to turn three and I was eleven. We, of course, were at a pageant. I was jealous of all the attention Mac was getting from Mom. So I went up to my mother and said, "Mama, I want to do pageants, too."

I know. *What was I thinking?*

I thought this would make Mom happy. Dad had been gone for over a year and it was clear he wasn't coming back. I figured it was something we all could do as a family. Plus, I wanted my mom to look at me the same way she looked at Mac. For her to be proud of me, like she was of her youngest child.

Mom looked me right in the eye and said, "Sweetie, pageants are for girls like your sister. You see how pretty those girls are. You'd be much better off concentrating on something you're good at, like telling jokes. Everybody thinks you're so funny. You've got a great personality, Lex. There's no need for you to try to be pretty." And then to add insult to injury, she looked me up and down and said, "You've got my genes, so no decent pageant gown would fit over your hips."

I went on a diet right then and there. Although I knew that losing a few pounds would never make me the pretty one. What was the point? Her rejection made me want to do the *opposite* of being in a pageant. So that meant no fancy hair, no makeup, no flashy clothes, nothing overly girly. And no pink, ever.

I've been confined by my mom's idea of me for so long, I almost forgot that I had the power to change myself. That I didn't have to be what my mom thought of me. I could be whatever I wanted to be.

But all of that is lost on Mom, because she's only concerned about Mac's happiness.

Even now as she looks at me, it's clear that she doesn't have a clue at how much her words had hurt me. How those words continue to haunt me. "You're being incredibly selfish, Lexi. All of your sister's hard work, and for what?"

And that's the million dollar question: *What's this all for?*

I look over and see Mackenzie in tears. I don't feel bad about preventing the show from filming us, but I do feel bad about making Mac cry. I kneel down to her. "Look, Mackenzie, I'm really sorry if you wanted to be on that show, but honestly, it would've been bad for you. I know I say things sometimes and I do think these pageants are a joke, but you're my little sister. I'm trying to look out for you."

She starts sobbing and I hold her. A wave of guilt encompasses my body. Maybe I should've kept my big mouth shut.

I hear Mac say something, but her mouth is up against my shoulder so I can't hear her.

I pull away. "What did you say?"

"It's okay, I didn't want to do it anyways. Madison still gets made fun of for the tantrum she threw on her show."

"Oh . . ."

I look up to see if this has changed Mom's attitude. But alas, she still looks like she's about to punch a hole through the wall.

Mackenzie goes over to her and puts her hand in Mom's. "Mama, I'm sorry you're mad, but I didn't want to do it."

Mom keeps looking at me in disgust. "You're not saying that to protect your sister, are you?"

Protect me from *what* exactly? Or I guess it's more of a *whom*.

Mac shakes her head. "I told you when you started filling out the application."

Mom starts walking. Both Mac and I follow behind her, not sure what else to do. For a brief moment, I'm hoping, wishing that Mac's admission might mean that Mom will drop it. That it is possible for her to listen to what her children are saying and realize that she's in the wrong.

Mom stops for a second and turns around to address me. "We're going. But let me make it clear that we are *not* finished with this."

16.

Two's a Date, Four's a Headache

I haven't yet decided if I like being given the silent treatment.

On the one hand, I get to come and go as I please. Mom barely acknowledges me. Which is weird because Mackenzie has made it clear she didn't want to be on the show. But I'm starting to think that for Mom the pageants aren't really about Mac.

On the other hand, I feel like a visitor in my own home. Every time I open the door, I brace myself for some sort of confrontation, but usually it's quiet. Mom has even stopped asking me to take Mac places. There's a pageant this weekend, and for the first time ever, I don't have to go. I've been hoping to get out of being the little errand girl for years, but now I feel like I truly don't belong here. I no longer have a place in my own home.

A line has been drawn. It's them versus me.

I pick up the phone. I've wanted to do this for years, but it seems like now is as good a time as any.

He answers after the second ring. "Hello?"

Hearing his voice instantly make me feel better. "Hey, Dad."

"Alexis! How's my little princess?"

I smile at the nickname Dad's had for me since I was little — a nickname that was given to me out of love, not a meaningless pageant title.

"I'm good. I was wondering if you wanted to come up this weekend. Mac and Mom have a pageant to go to and I'll have the house to myself on Saturday. Or I could come to you?"

A red envelope on the end table catches my eye. I pick it up and see FINAL NOTICE written on it.

"Lexi?"

I didn't hear anything that he just said. I place the overdue bill back where it was. "Um, sorry, what did you say?"

"I was just saying that I can't believe you'd rather see your old man than throw a big raging party while you're home alone!"

Yeah, well, I'm lame. And I don't want people to see where I live. So I guess that makes me double lame.

"Of course I'd rather see you. Plus, I got my fake ID taken away after a bar fight last weekend, so no way to get a keg."

I hear his laughter on the other end. "Oh, I've missed you, princess. Why don't we meet halfway?"

A parent with some sense.

About time.

It has finally happened.

I'm on a date with Logan Reeves. It's what I always dreamed of.

Okay, to be honest, in my dreams, his girlfriend wasn't there. And I wasn't with someone else, either.

But really, that's just petty semantics.

I can't help but smile to myself as the four of us sit at Mario's Pizza.

Alyssa puts down her menu. "You guys get whatever you want. I'm only having a salad."

I know that I can be annoying about food, but I'm the type of person who likes to splurge on special occasions. And this is definitely a special occasion. So unlike Sprouts Queen, I will be having pizza with the boys. A guy has got to like a girl who doesn't eat like a rabbit.

At least I hope Logan does.

And Taylor.

Who I'm here with.

As if he can sense my thoughts, Taylor puts his arm around me. "Anything special you want on the pizza?"

"Nope, whatever you guys want." I smile back at him. I wonder if seeing us together is making Logan jealous.

"So let's get pepperoni —"

"Oh, wait, I don't eat meat on pizza." So much for being the low-maintenance one.

"Are you a vegetarian?" Alyssa asks.

"No, I just don't like meat on pizza. It's weird, I know. I . . . It's no big deal, I can pick it off."

Taylor shakes his head. "We can order half without meat."

"Thanks."

I study Taylor's profile. He really is hot. And sweet. And kinda perfect.

So why exactly can't I stop thinking about Logan, who now has his hand on Alyssa's knee? And why does Alyssa look bored by all of this? Does she not realize how lucky she is?

Alyssa's bag starts to vibrate. "Sorry!" she says as she digs through her large red purse. "It's my pageant coach, be right back!"

Alyssa excuses herself, leaving me with Logan. And Taylor. Yes, Taylor.

"I hope it's good news." Logan stares out the window to where Alyssa is talking animatedly into her phone. "She's been really stressed-out lately and not acting like herself. Everybody says she's a shoo-in for Miss Teen Dallas this year, which means the Miss Teen Texas pageant this summer." He crosses his fingers.

I burst out laughing.

He gives me a confused look. "What?"

I purse my lips and shake my head.

"C'mon!" He smiles at me. And I know it shouldn't. I know I'm here with Taylor (I really do), but my heart still melts.

"Nothing. You sound exactly like a proud pageant mom."

Logan looks at me in horror. "You did *not* just say that to me."

"I only speak the truth. I mean, *maybe* I've caught you lip-synching to Alyssa's talent song once . . . or forty times. Somewhere in that range — I'm not a hundred percent sure."

Logan throws his napkin as me. "Like you don't have your sister's routine memorized. Unless you can't booty pop like a seven-year-old."

"Oh, I can booty pop. Trust me, Mackenzie learns *all* her moves from me."

He raises his eyebrow. "I'm sure she does."

"See, it seems like you're mocking me, but at least *I'm* not a seventeen-year-old boy spending my weekends at beauty pageants, watching underage girls perform scandalous routines. I believe there are words for someone like you."

"I think the word you're looking for is *stud*."

"Oh, that's interesting, I was thinking more along the lines of a *pedophile*."

"Do not compare me to Mr. Norman."

"Eww!" I scream.

Logan covers his face up. "Can you believe that no one says anything when he sits back and records the toddlers?"

"And what deranged 'talent agency' would have someone like that represent them?"

"Does anybody fall for that?"

Now it's time for me to cover my face. "My *mom* took his business card."

Logan slams his hand on the table. "No, she did not! And by 'business card,' do you mean an old receipt with his number on it?"

"Wait, is that not how legitimate businessmen behave? So that guy who had this really cool van in the parking lot isn't going to put me in his movie? *He said I had potential!*"

"What did I miss?" Alyssa sits back down.

Suddenly, reality comes crashing down around me.

Alyssa looks around the restaurant. "Where's Taylor?"

Taylor's not here? When did he leave the table?

"He's, um . . ." I look at Logan, who simply shrugs his shoulders. I excuse myself from the table and head toward the restroom, hoping to see Taylor on my way. I find him sitting on a bench near the entrance.

"Hey," I say, "I was wondering where you went off to."

He looks up at me and the warmness that was on his face just a few minutes ago is gone. "Oh, so you realized that I was at the table."

"Of course, I knew —"

He cuts me off. "What was that with Logan?"

I sit down next to him. "I'm really sorry, it's silly inside pageant stuff. I didn't mean to exclude you — it's what we do to get through those agonizing weekends."

"Yeah, looks like *torture*."

I don't know what to say. Of course I had to mess this up. *Of course*. I mean, yeah, for a split second I thought I was on a date with Logan, but what I did wasn't fair to Taylor. I should've known better. He deserves better.

And maybe I do, too. Maybe I should stop pining after someone who (a) isn't available and (b) clearly isn't interested. Especially when I have someone right here in front of me who's pretty great.

"Listen." I place my hand on his knee. "If you want, we can go back to my house and I can make my sister perform her entire pageant routine. You really haven't lived until you've seen a seven-year-old dance to 'It's Raining Men' with an umbrella and glitter. It really is spectacular."

I see the corner of his mouth turn up.

"And I'm sure if we ask really nicely, she can lend you one of her crowns so you can experience what it's like to be superior. I think you'd look great with a faux diamond tiara on your forehead."

I've got a full smile from him now. He shakes his head. "Sorry about that. It was weird, I felt like I was the third wheel. I guess maybe I should've thought of something else for us to do on our second *real* date since I'm clearly not ready to share you yet."

"We'll make up an excuse after pizza and go somewhere, just the two of us."

He leans in. "That sounds like a plan."

Butterflies start circling my stomach as Taylor doesn't drop his gaze. And I don't want to turn away. He takes my chin in the palm of his hand and draws me closer to him. Our lips touch and I close my eyes.

The fact that we're in the middle of a restaurant doesn't bother me because all I can feel is his warm lips on mine.

When we finally part, the fact that we *are* in public causes my cheeks to burn.

"Oh, hey, man." I follow Taylor's gaze to find Logan staring at us with wide eyes.

He scratches his head and motions toward the table. "Yeah, um, wanted you to know the pizza's here."

"Cool." Taylor nods at Logan. Logan pauses for a minute before he heads back to Alyssa.

Taylor turns to me with a crooked smile. "Sorry." He tucks a stray piece of hair behind my ear. "I couldn't help myself. Next time, I'll make sure we're totally alone. Sound good?"

I nod, but can't hide a ridiculous smile that's spreading across my face.

I finally had my first kiss. And it was good. Very, very good.

And the fact that Logan walked in on it?

Even better.

17.

A Thin Line Between Friendship and Abandonment

'll admit that I always thought it was ridiculous when you'd read a book or listen to a song and a girl would say that she would practically float after a kiss.

And okay, I'll further confess that I used to think that about when Logan and I would have our first kiss.

But then I had my first kiss.

And it was amazing.

My stomach keeps flipping every time I think about that first kiss . . . and our second one later that night that lasted much longer. How I didn't want the evening to end. How I didn't want the kiss to end.

How I don't want this whole fairy tale I've created to end. Because my clock has to strike midnight at some point. Doesn't it?

"Hello, heartbreaker!" Benny greets me at lunch on Thursday.

I can't help but burst into a fit of girlish giggles. So yes, it appears that I'm every inch the girly girl I used to make fun of (but secretly envied).

"Hey, Lexi!" Hannah comes over. "I love your necklace."

"Thanks!"

She gives me a genuine smile. "See you later!"

Benny and Cam exchange a look. "See you later?" Cam asks.

"Oh, yeah. Hannah, Josh, Taylor, and I are going to grab a quick bite before I have to work tonight." I try to hide my excitement from them, knowing full well they'll be unhappy about my increasing time with "the dark side."

"We're still on for tomorrow night?" Benny asks for the eleventh time.

"Of course," I confirm. "Just so you know, Taylor asked me out but I told him that I had plans. And you guys know I hardly ever have a Friday night off, but I'd never ditch you guys." So there's still a part of Fiercely Loyal Lexi behind this giddy exterior.

"Gee, thanks," Cam says dryly.

Given Cam's response, I decide not to tell them that I've also refused Taylor's invite to sit with him and the other Chosen Ones at lunch. I don't think they'd appreciate it as much as they should. But I gave them my word, and good friends keep their promises.

"Hey, Lexi!" Taylor comes up to our table and kisses me on the cheek. I can't believe he did that in the cafeteria. That's like the most public display of affection you can do at school. "I brought you dessert." He hands me a brownie.

"Thanks!" I usually don't eat dessert, but I'm pretty sure that I heard that kissing burns calories, so . . . "Do you want to join us?" I know that I'm not allowed to go join him, but I don't see the reason why he can't hang out with us.

"Yeah, awesome!" He runs over to grab his lunch from the Beautiful People's table.

"That's okay, right?" I ask Benny and Cam.

"Oh, I'll ask Chris!" Benny gets up and goes over to Chris's table.

"I can't believe how well things are going, you know?" I say to Cam. She gives me a weak smile.

"Hey, guys, what's up?" Taylor says as he sits down next to me.

Benny brings over Chris and proudly introduces him to Taylor.

As soon as we all settle in, there's some silence. Cam, Benny, and I aren't used to having company, especially of the cute-boy variety.

"I'm thinking of making a 'Please Don't Go, Lexi' T-shirt for tomorrow night," Benny announces.

"Where are you going?" Taylor asks. "Or is this your way of dumping me?"

I give Benny the death stare. He mouths "sorry" to me. "It's nothing," I say with a shrug of my shoulders. "I'm meeting my father this weekend and discussing my living arrangements."

I haven't been thinking that much about the conversation I need to have with my father, mostly because I'm in denial that I might have to move to Houston if I want to be with him. Ideally, my dad would move back here, but I don't think that's going to happen. But I can't keep living at home, where Mom *tolerates* me being there. I can't keep it up for another eighteen months.

I decide to distract Taylor. "Oh, tell them the story about your parents' honeymoon. It's *so* funny."

Thankfully, Taylor doesn't ask any more questions. He starts telling this hysterical story about his parents' honeymoon where everything and anything that could possibly go wrong does go wrong, including getting stuck for five extra days due to a hurricane.

I study Taylor as he animates the story with hand gestures and different voices. Benny and Chris are laughing along, clearly approving of my choice in male companions. But I notice Cam quietly eating her lunch, politely smiling and nodding. I've known her for years, so it's clear to me that she isn't the least bit interested in anything Taylor has to say.

"You're hysterical," Benny says to Taylor after he's finished. He gives me a little wink. "You should totally come over to my house tomorrow night. We're having movie night. Chris is coming."

He is? This is *insane*. I can't help but grin looking at us. Here Benny and I are with boyfriends.

"Yes!" I don't know why I didn't think about inviting him before. "You're going to die when you see Benny's house. It's *ah*-mazing."

A small sound escapes Cam's mouth, but I ignore her.

"I'd love to," Taylor says as he puts his arm around me.

"But be careful with that one," Benny warns Taylor. "Sure she looks all sweet and innocent, but get her on a Ms. Pac-Man game and she'll tear your limb off if you so much as talk to her while she's playing."

"You were *distracting* me on purpose," I defend myself.

"He does like to do that, huh?" Chris says, nudging Benny playfully.

I can't get over how the four of us are bantering back and forth like we've known one another for years. I try to get Cam involved in the conversation, but she just gives one-word answers. She excuses herself early, citing some test she has to study for.

Chris and Taylor don't know any better, but I know Cam. She never leaves anything early to go study.

But I'll get to the bottom of that later. Right now, I'm enjoying my little double date.

Cam's waiting by my locker after school. I don't even bother to give her much of a smile, because I'm not over how rude she was to Taylor at lunch. And I have a feeling that tomorrow night will be even more awkward.

"Hey," she says quietly.

"Hey," I reply back, waiting for her apology.

"So, I don't think I'm going to come to Benny's tomorrow night." She folds her arms like she's making some sort of stand.

"Why don't you like Taylor?" I blurt out.

She gives me a weird look. "I don't dislike Taylor," she tells me. Or at least that's what her mouth says; her eyes are telling me a different story.

"Yes, you do." I haven't been a fan of some of the guys Cam's been into, but I've kept my mouth shut until she's been ready to hear what I have to say. Usually I don't even need to say a word — the second the guy does something jerky, she dumps him.

She lets out a little sigh. "Honestly, I don't have any problems with Taylor. He *seems* like a good guy." I grimace at her. "But I have to admit that I do question his motives."

She's lost me. "What do you mean *motives*?"

"He never really paid much attention to you, and then you become a fancy version of yourself and suddenly you seem to matter. It's a little insulting."

"Well, what do you want me to do? Do you want me to show up in sweats and no makeup and see how he reacts? Did you ever think that maybe I like to dress up? That I like to wear makeup?"

To be honest, I don't like to wear *this* much makeup. But I've started to get breakouts from using all these different products on my face. So now I need *more* makeup to cover up the red bumps and splotches. It's a vicious cycle.

I find myself getting increasingly upset at Cam, and a little out of sorts because what she said is *technically* true. Taylor didn't pay attention to me until I glammed up. But so what? I was a drab version of myself — why would he want to be with someone like that? It's no wonder guys would never give me the time of day.

"I can't believe that you, out of all people, aren't happy for me." I point my finger accusingly at her. "I'm finally out of this rut I've been in for years. Because this is more like how I used to be before everything in my life flipped upside down. Dad left. Mom got fat. I got a bratty sister. And, let's face it, I gave up on thinking that anything good would happen to me, that I could get what I want. I went through the motions. I thought my only hope for happiness was to move to New York. So really, who gives a flying crap if I want to wear some makeup and try to look nice?" My voice cracks and I realize that I'm on the verge of tears.

Cam takes a defensive step back. "I do realize what you've been through and how hard things have been for you." She steps forward and holds my hand. "Please don't be upset. I have no problem with what you're doing. I think you need to do whatever makes you feel better. And I'm sorry, I shouldn't have said anything about Taylor. He really does seem nice."

I feel awful. I shouldn't have snapped at Cam. Both she and Benny have been nothing but supportive of me through everything I've been through. And not just Post-Makeover Lexi. They're the ones who've been by my side through all the family drama and breakdowns.

"Please come tomorrow night," I say. I know I thought it would be awkward with her, but now it would be even more awkward without her.

Plus, if she spent more time with Taylor and me, then maybe she'd see that there's more substance to our relationship than merely looks.

Cam looks down at the floor. "I'd feel like a fifth wheel."

Lexi, you idiot.

I've been so focused on me and *my* life that I never once stopped and considered how Cam feels with all these changes.

"I'm so sorry, Cam, I didn't think . . ."

She waves me away. "It's totally fine, Lex. Yeah, I feel a little left out, but I'm happy for you and Benny, I really am. I just think that maybe you guys would have a better time without me."

"That's not possible."

She gives me a genuine smile. "Really, it's fine. I want you guys to have fun, and this way I can get my parents off my back and babysit so they can have a night out. It's totally fine. You're going to have a great time, and I can't wait to hear all about it."

I so don't deserve Cam. She's never once canceled plans on me when she's had a boyfriend and what do I do? I've been dating a guy for a couple weeks and I've already made her feel left out.

"I'm seeing my dad on Saturday and have to work on Sunday, but let's do something on Monday. Just the two of us. Okay?"

Cam agrees and, yet again, assures me that she's okay. But I feel like I've let her down. I did the one pageant thing I swore I'd never do: *Step on whoever to get to the top.*

18.

The Family Ties That Break

I can't believe that this is my life. This evening with Benny, Chris, and Taylor feels like a dream.

I was a little nervous that Taylor wouldn't be cool with Benny and Chris being together. I know Benny was being cautious so his parents wouldn't think anything was going on, but as soon as we got to the game room, Chris took Benny's hand, and it's remained there for most of the evening. If Taylor's uncomfortable, he's not showing it. I didn't realize how his approval would make me so happy. I couldn't be with anybody who didn't fully accept Benny for who he is.

We were supposed to watch a movie, but there hasn't been a lull in the conversation. Everything flows like we've been hanging out for years. I don't know why I'm so surprised to find out that Taylor has a lot in common with Benny and Chris. Taylor likes the same role-playing video game that Chris is into, and they've already made plans to play it this weekend. And Benny's thrilled because Taylor also has an affinity for some old TV show about some guy who can diffuse a bomb with, like, a paper clip and duct tape. (Taylor's aunt gave him the DVDs for his birthday last year and he's apparently become obsessed.) I'm so excited to have Benny and Taylor engaged in such an enthusiastic conversation that I keep smiling and nodding . . . and apparently agree to watch a marathon next weekend.

This is one thing Benny and I do not see eye to eye on (and apparently now Taylor as well): All these old shows make me laugh. Everybody's hair is like two feet high, and they're all wearing shoulder pads and high-waisted pants. I'm so distracted by their outfits, I can't pay attention to anything that's coming out of their mouths.

Taylor doesn't even mind that I *may* be insinuating that he's a wimp when he lets Benny score two points against us while playing air hockey. Luckily, I'm able to subsequently crush Chris and earn the nickname Killer, which I'll wear proudly. *Somebody* has to show the boys how it's done.

Despite the fact that none of us wants the evening to end, the reality of my approaching curfew forces us to get ready to leave. Taylor holds my jacket open for me, while I see Benny do the same for Chris. I smile at something that's foreign to us both, yet familiar at the same time.

It's all so perfect.

Well, truthfully it would be perfect if Cam were here. I know she thought it would be weird for her to come, but it's not the same without her. Like there's a part of me missing.

Chris gives each of us a hug as we say good-bye for the evening. "I don't know about you, but I don't think there's a better way to start off the weekend." I couldn't agree more. I wish all Fridays could be like tonight. "What's everybody up to tomorrow?"

Tomorrow.

My nearly perfect existence comes crashing down as I realize that I have to confront the biggest void in my life — my father.

The next morning, I get excited at each passing mile marker on the road to our meeting point, halfway between Dallas and Houston. I haven't seen Dad in over two months. He only lives four hours away in Houston, but it might as well be Hawaii.

Whenever I haven't seen him in a long time, it's uncomfortable at first, almost like we're strangers. He asks politely about school, work, and whatever fashion project I'm working on that week. I ask him questions about his work and life, and he's always really vague. Like I'm too young to understand his life. I don't know, maybe I am, but sometimes I wish it was like it used to be. Before Mackenzie was born. Before Mom became unreasonable.

When we were a family.

Not only am I excited to see Dad alone, but I can't wait for him to meet Lexi 2.0. Back when I was Daddy's Little Girl, I used to wear pretty cotton dresses and have ribbons in my hair. I was his little princess and the apple of his eye. I loved going to his office to bring him lunch: I could make a mean peanut-butter-and-jelly sandwich when I was little. All his coworkers would fuss over me, tell me how adorable I was.

And then everything changed.

I shake off the negative thoughts as I pull into the parking lot of the café where we're meeting. I see Dad's car is already there. I practically run up the stairs to the door. I see Dad waiting for me at a corner table.

He looks up at me as I approach, gives me a slight smile, looks back at his menu . . . and then his head shoots right back up.

"Lexi?" Dad jumps up out of his chair and comes over to hug me. "Lexi, my princess, look at you! I almost didn't recognize you!" He holds out his hands and twirls me around. "You look fantastic, sweetheart!"

"Thanks, Dad. I missed you."

He gives me another hug. "Aww, I missed you, too." He gestures toward the table for me to sit down.

"What's going on with you? How's school? How are Cameron and Benny?"

"It's all really great, Dad."

"I'm so happy for you, Lexi. I've got some news for you."

"Really?"

Please say you're moving back to Dallas. Please say you're moving back to Dallas.

I've been holding on to this fantasy that one day he'd move back near us since he first walked out the door of our old house. I really don't think I can stand living with Mom any longer. I want to move in with my dad. I want to start feeling like I belong somewhere. Like I have a home where I'm wanted.

I hold my breath for Dad's big news.

He shifts uncomfortably in his seat. "I've been wondering when a good time would be to tell you, but I've . . . I've met somebody."

And all I can think is: *What?*

Followed by: *How?*

And then, as I am one-thousandth of the way to comprehending this: *Who?*

I don't know why I'm so shocked. My dad's a good-looking guy. It's funny because I never really noticed any changes in my father growing up. But once I stopped seeing him on a daily basis, I started to notice the flecks of gray in his brown hair, the wrinkles that have started to form around his green eyes. Despite the signs of aging, his face is still slightly boyish. And of course there's that smile, one that slowly came back after the separation. Now he's beaming. Because he has someone new in his life.

He's still waiting for my reaction.

"Um," I say, "that's great." I guess that's what you're supposed to say when your father tells you he's dating someone. I have no idea. I assume he's dated since the divorce, but he's never mentioned it before.

He goes on. "Maybe you can spend a weekend next month with us. I'd really like you to meet her."

"I'd —"

Something hits me. He said that I should spend it with *us*.

It clicks. The *Where?*

"Are you living together?" I ask.

Dad studies me carefully before he nods. "She moved in a couple weeks ago. I planned on telling you about Kurstin during your last visit, but it got canceled."

"Does Mom know?"

He shakes his head. "No. I didn't want to tell you until it was serious."

Oh. It was serious enough for them to move in together, but not to tell his oldest child?

"How long have you been dating?"

He's got a huge smile on his face. "About six months."

Six months? This person has been a part of my dad's life for *six months* and he's neglected to mention it to me. Am I even a part of his life anymore? I know I should be happy for him, but I can't help but feel like I'm losing the last member of my family.

"Listen to me!" He laughs. "I'm telling you everything about me, but what about you? Anybody special in your life?"

"No."

What's the point of me telling him about Taylor? I figure I'll wait until I get engaged and call him up and say, *"Hey, Dad, so wanted to see if you'd be interested in coming up next weekend since I'm getting married."*

Of course my lack of a boyfriend is not news to Dad, so he doesn't skip a beat. "Well, you'll find someone special someday, Lex. You're bright and have such a great personality."

Are you even kidding me right now?

This whole day is turning out to be the exact opposite of what I wanted and needed. I decide to talk about the only subject that can't be ruined: my future.

"Have you talked to Uncle Pat recently about New York?"

Dad's brother lives in Stamford, Connecticut, and the plan is for me to stay with him this summer during the FIT program.

"Yes, he's really excited to have you."

At least I still have this going for me.

"Although . . ." My heart jumps into my throat. That "although" doesn't sound like it's good news. ". . . your mother is a little worried about the costs involved with the trip."

I feel my entire body tense up. "I'm paying my own way. I have enough for my plane ticket, registration, supplies, mass transit, food. . . ."

Dad smiles at me. "I know you do. I guess she's concerned that maybe it's too expensive and you should be saving your money for something else."

"Like what? Dresses for Mackenzie? A new set of dentures for her seven-year-old mouth? More hairpieces? More photos?" I throw my menu down. We haven't even had a chance to order lunch yet, and we're already on my least favorite topic.

"Whoa." Dad pats my hand. "No one is saying you should spend your money on your sister."

No one at this table.

"Look." Dad picks up my menu and hands it back to me. "Let's order some food and then talk about whatever else you want to talk about. We don't have to talk about the pageants, money, or your mother. This is our time together, I don't want anything to ruin it."

Yeah, too late.

Plus, what I want to talk to him about has to do with pageants, money, and Mom. I figure it's time to go for broke.

"Sorry, it's just . . . things are pretty bad at home. And that's what I kind of wanted to talk to you about."

Dad leans in, and for a second I think I see a flash of panic in his eyes.

He gives me a slight smile. "I know it's rough, but things will get better. Your sister can't do pageants forever. She'll grow out of it."

There's a tightness in my chest. I didn't realize how much I need him to save me from my current circumstance. I need him to see it my way, for him to understand. "It's not just the pageants. I mean, I guess it is, but mostly it's Mom. I don't really feel like I belong there. I was hoping . . ."

I look right in my dad's eyes and he looks away. I can already tell what he's going to say before he even opens his mouth.

"Lexi, you know I love you." He fidgets with the straw in his water. "But it's not a good time right now. Kurstin just moved in, you're in the middle of a semester. Let's see how the next few months play out."

He motions for the waitress to come and take our order, but I no longer have an appetite. I'm stuck.

There's no way out.

19.

When the Going Gets Tough, the Tough Wear Rouge

I'm in desperate need of an aspirin. My head has been throbbing since I left Dad. When I pull up to our house, I see Mom's car parked in the driveway. I let out a little groan. The last thing I wanted to come back to was them gloating about whatever pageant they just attended.

I open up the front door to find Mackenzie watching TV while eating ice cream.

"Hey."

"Hi." She looks up. "How's Dad?"

"Good," I lie. Okay, technically Dad's wonderful. He's great. Only he doesn't want to have his daughter come live with him. Oh, and he has a live-in girlfriend. One small fact Dad has asked me to keep from Mom and Mac until he's ready to tell them. While I'm not happy to have yet another thing pulling me further apart from them (as I'll be living here for a while now), I know that this would put Mom over the edge.

I sit down next to Mac. "He sends his love. Where's Mom?"

"In her room."

"How did the pageant go?"

She sets her bowl down. "It went okay — second place. I totally rocked beauty. Then I botched my talent routine. I was in the middle of my 'I Want Candy' dance routine and, I don't know, the routine left me. I threw out the candy too early and my cartwheel wasn't straight and I sorta froze. Mom was totally stressed-out."

I see some paperwork next to her and pick it up.

"Oh, that's for next weekend's pageant," she says with a hint of annoyance.

It's the form the emcees use to introduce each contestant. I start to read it aloud: "Mackenzie has blond hair and blue eyes. When she grows up, she wants to be Miss America. Her favorite food is macaroni and cheese. Her favorite subject is math, and her best friend is her mother."

"Mom wrote that." She looks tired. Too tired for someone her age.

"Figured." I nudge her knee playfully with mine.

We hear Mom's voice calling out from her bedroom. "Who's that? Is Lexi home?"

"Yes," I shout.

She comes out. "Oh. How's your father?"

"Good." I hope she won't press me on the subject.

"That's good." Mom studies me and it's almost like she can tell I'm holding something back. "What did you talk about?"

"Ah, stuff . . ." I hesitate. She's never asked details before. I wonder if she knows about the new woman. And if she now knows that I know. Is this a test? "Um, he wants both Mac and me to come up in a few weekends."

Mac's face lights up. "Can we, Mama?"

"I'll check the pageant schedule."

Mackenzie sinks down into the couch. "I'd rather see Dad than go to another pageant."

Mom waves her finger at Mac. "Well, maybe if you spent more time thinking about the pageant, you wouldn't botch your routines."

I shoot Mom a look. All Mac does is work on the pageants. I don't think I could remember all the different routines she has: beauty, talent, western wear, outfit of choice, parade of desperation. . . . (Okay, I *may* have made one of those up.)

"Did your sister tell you what happened? It was a complete disaster. She totally lost her feet."

I look over and see tears welling in Mac's eyes.

I grab her feet. "Looks like she found them again. Phew, that would've been rough."

Corny, I know. But Mac smiles.

Mom, however, is not amused. She studies me for a few beats. I contemplate telling her the truth. I don't see why I have to be put in yet another awkward position with her by holding back. And when Dad does finally decide to tell her, he'll probably let it slip that I already know.

I open my mouth, then close it again. Today has not turned out as I had hoped, and the last thing I want is for Mom to take this news out on me. I had to deal with the back-and-forth during the divorce, hearing my mom say awful things about my father. Mac's too young to remember, but unfortunately I'll never be able to forget the screaming, the accusations of lies, the fighting.

"Is there something you want to say?" Mom stands over me.

"No," I lie.

She storms back into her room muttering something under her breath.

Mac sits back up. "Are you going out with Cam and Benny tonight?"

I shake my head.

"Taylor?"

"No. I wasn't sure when I'd get back."

Mac walks over to the entertainment cabinet and pulls out a DVD. "Do you want to watch *The Muppets* with me?"

"Honestly, Mac, there's nothing else I'd rather do right now."

And oddly enough, that's the absolute truth.

I'm headed to lunch on Monday when I see Taylor in an intense conversation with Logan and Alyssa.

"Hey, guys," I say as I cautiously approach them. I'm still not used to being part of their circle, so I never really feel like I belong.

"It's a disaster!" Alyssa exclaims.

Logan puts his arm around her and kisses her on the lips. What is with him anyways? Why does he feel the need to kiss or touch her at every opportunity? I mean, Taylor and I kiss, but in private. Well, most of the time.

I try to shake off the jealous feeling that's overwhelming me. I thought that as Taylor and I got more serious I'd stop obsessing over Logan, but old habits (and delusional fantasies) die hard.

Strangely, Alyssa doesn't seem comfortable with the kiss, either. She never seems as excited about Logan's affections as I would be, or any other sane girl (well, maybe not so sane in my case).

"Is everything okay?" I ask.

Alyssa juts her bottom lip out. "I just realized the booster dinner is the same night as my preliminary pageant for Miss Teen Dallas. So not fair."

I guess it's a beauty-pageant thing to think that everything and everybody is out to get you. How could the athletic department not check the pageant schedule before setting a date for the night when all the athletes get feted at a dinner in their honor? How rude of them.

I've only heard rumors about the booster dinner. It's allegedly for all of the athletic teams at school, but most of the focus is on the football team. Just another ego boost to a group of people who don't need it. I've always wanted to go, though, because I really am that pathetic. There's a dance afterward for the attendees, and it's all anybody can talk about the week after. Cam went to it once when she dated Jeremy, since he was on the football team. I, of course, have never been asked to go. Yet.

But wait. If Alyssa isn't going to be there . . .

Logan wraps his arms around her. "It's only a stupid dinner. You've been working so hard for this. I'm just going to hang with my guys and keep my fingers crossed for you."

"I know." Alyssa shrugs her shoulder, like Logan's arm is uncomfortable (*jealousy, table of one!*). "Nothing is going to get in my way. Nothing."

So that means . . .

Logan looks at Taylor. "You don't mind if I crash with you at the dance?"

"Sure." Taylor nods. "Lexi and I can slum it with you."

Wait. *What?* I guess this means that I'm going . . . and that Logan will be alone.

Of course, all of this is lost on Taylor because he's so nice. I really don't deserve him.

Alyssa looks slightly relieved. "Thanks, guys."

As if Logan would be lost without her.

Stop it, Lexi.

"Hey, Lexi." Alyssa looks sweetly at me. "Promise me you'll throw Logan a bone and dance one song with him."

What the *what?*

She leans in. "You and Logan are such good friends; it would make me feel better knowing that he wasn't going to be completely lonely the entire night, especially since you're *such good friends.*"

Yes, I get that Logan and I are "such good friends." Thank you for reminding me for the millionth time.

Logan also seems to be annoyed at Alyssa's use of the phrase. He's certainly noticed it. He puts his arm down, clearly done with his attempts to comfort her.

I stammer, "Oh, well . . . Yeah, I guess . . . Um." All three of them are staring at me since I'm completely unable to form a complete sentence. "I, ah, better head over to my table."

"You should join us," Alyssa offers.

"Thanks, but I'm going to go . . ." *to where it isn't this confusing.*

"You want me to join?" Taylor wraps an arm around me.

I think of Cam. "Would you mind if it's just me, Cam, and Benny? I feel like I need to focus on them a bit."

"Of course." He kisses me on the forehead. "As long as I get to have you all to myself tomorrow night."

I excuse myself and head to my regular table. I talked to Benny last night and he's having Chris sit elsewhere as well. I think it's important for us to have a few lunches where it's only the three of us. And I'm extremely grateful that we're doing it today, since I'm having a crisis of conscience.

"What's the latest drama with the Beautiful People?" Benny asks as I sit down.

"Oh, it's . . . I think I'm an awful person."

"What?" Benny and Cam ask in unison.

"Why can't I get Logan out of my head?"

"Because you're a glutton for punishment," Benny says with a grin.

"Clearly." I open up my lunch, but I'm not even hungry. I push it aside.

Cam leans in. "What's wrong?"

"Nothing . . ." I fill them in on the latest developments. "I should be jumping for joy that I'm with somebody as amazing as Taylor, but now all I can think about is that Logan is going to be there. And that he might dance with me."

"You know," Benny says, serious now, "we've often joked about doing a Loganvention on you and it seems like you may really need one."

I nod. "I do, I really do."

"Truer words have never been spoken," Cam says with a nod.

"Okay, repeat after me." Benny is clearly enjoying this more than he should. "I, Alexis Anderson, do solemnly swear . . ." He gestures at me.

"Do you seriously want me —"

"*Do solemnly swear . . .*"

I give in. I so deserve this right now. "I, Alexis Anderson, do solemnly swear . . ."

Benny continues. "To focus on my hot boyfriend and stop obsessing over Logan. I will not stalk his profile page, take different routes between classes so I 'accidentally' bump into him, delay packing my backpack so I can 'coincidentally' walk to the parking lot at the same time as him, or invent any other activity that's invented solely to spend time with him."

Wow. This is embarrassing. And it's all true. *All of it.*

Benny gestures his hands at me.

"Um, what you said."

"And no talking about him anymore. I've got a movie date with Chris tonight, so, Cam, you're on duty."

She rubs her hands together. "Oh, this is going to be good."

Yeah, for one of us.

20.

For Whom the Cash Register Tolls

O n my way to meet Cam after school, I run to the bank to put my paycheck into my savings account. I always have a feeling of accomplishment every time I make a deposit. I love seeing the money grow and grow. And when I see my ATM receipt, I don't just see dollars and cents. I see my future.

I take the receipt and my smile quickly vanishes.

My head is cloudy as I try to make sense of the numbers. It's suddenly as if I'm reading a foreign language.

Something is wrong.

Something is terribly, terribly wrong.

I feel bile start to rise in my throat and I quickly swallow in hopes of keeping the sick feeling from taking over me. There's no way this can be happening.

Over four thousand dollars is gone from my account.

I run inside the bank and see several people in line. How did my account get hacked? Where did the money go? My mind starts racing with all those ads on TV for identify theft. Maybe that's what happened to me. But how could that have happened? Who would want to be me?

It has taken me nearly three years to save up that money, including working all summer and babysitting on my days off. And now it's gone, just like that.

I think I'm going to have a nervous breakdown in line. I keep staring at the clock on the wall, hoping that it can provide an answer for me. But time seems to be standing still. I stare at the hands of the clock, willing them (and me) forward. I start clinging to the hope that the reason the line is taking forever is because there's a computer glitch that accidentally took four grand from everybody's account. I've got to cling to something. Since I really have nothing.

Finally, it's my turn.

"How can I help you?" a very tired-looking woman behind the counter asks.

My shaking hand gives her the receipt. "There seems to be an issue with my savings account. I know that I have way more money than this. I think I'm missing about four thousand dollars."

She looks at me suspiciously over her glasses. I give her my bank card and photo ID. She starts typing furiously on her keyboard. I try to remain calm, but I feel like I'm going to pass out.

She examines the screen for a few minutes. "According to our files, you took out four thousand dollars last Thursday."

"No, I didn't."

She glares at me. "Here's the withdrawal slip."

She turns her monitor so I can see the slip, made out for four grand.

And signed by my mother.

My.

Mother.

I try to find my voice. "That's not my signature. That's my mom, she . . ."

She couldn't have. She wouldn't.

But she did.

The woman gives me a tentative smile and pats my hand. "You have a joint account since you're a minor. You needed your mom to co-sign for it when you opened it up. It allows her access to the account."

I turn around in a daze and hear her call out for the next person in line.

I feel the tears streaming down my face as I force each step to get to my car. Once I get inside, I collapse in sobs over the steering wheel.

All the disappointment that I thought I felt, all the frustrations I thought I had, they're nothing compared to this one moment.

I'm devastated.

I'm lost.

I don't know what to do.

Everything's ruined.

I have no future.

Nothing.

It was all taken away from me with one signature.

I drive straight to the SuperStore. I've never bothered Mom while she's at work, but since she has zero respect for me, I don't have the slightest desire to show her any.

I'm aware that I'm borderline hysterical as I run through the aisles and aisles of every product you can name before I reach the customer service desk. Mom smiles as she sees me approaching, until she realizes that I look like I'm about to commit a murder.

"I need to take a break," she says over her shoulder to nobody in particular.

"HOW COULD YOU?" I scream at her. I don't care about making a scene. I don't care about anything right now, just getting what belongs to me. What I've *earned*.

"Lexi, lower your voice." She grabs my arm and pulls me into a tight back room filled with boxes.

I start to sob. "You stole from me. How could you steal from your own daughter? I can't go to New York now. I can't do anything. And it's all your fault."

"Stop being so dramatic. It was simply a loan." She folds her arms, like this is all just an inconvenience to her. Like she didn't ruin my life.

I look up at her, my own mother. The only feeling inside me is contempt. "A LOAN? You took it without my permission. And how the hell are *you* going to repay *me*?"

"Watch your language," she says curtly.

I'm shaking with anger. "You're really not in any position to start judging people, Mom."

"You're acting like a spoiled brat."

I get in her face. "I'm acting like a spoiled brat. Really? *I'm* the spoiled brat in this family? Who was the money you *stole* from me for?"

She pushes me away. "You're being unreasonable, Alexis. I was getting final notices. They were going to shut off the electricity. Last time I checked, you used the electricity in the house, didn't you? And the TV?"

"And why don't you have the money for the electricity?"

"That is none of your business, young lady." I see Mom ball her hands into tight fists.

I can hardly see straight, I'm filled with so much anger. All I can think to do is yell, "YOU MADE IT MY BUSINESS WHEN YOU STOLE FROM ME!"

"Look." Mom tries to steady her breath. "We needed some new things, the flipper and dresses for state preliminaries in a couple weeks. This is the big leagues, and that means money. We'll be able to pay you back when Mackenzie wins."

I can see in her eyes that she truly believes that all our troubles will go away if Mac takes home a big trophy. "And what if she doesn't?"

She clicks her tongue in disgust. "Get over yourself, Lexi. You know, it would be nice if just for once you had some faith in your little sister."

I can't believe this. "Just like the faith you have in your *other* daughter. You make me sick."

Before I realize it, the wind's knocked out of me. I try to steady my breathing as I adjust my head, which had been suddenly jerked to the side. A stinging sensation burns my face.

It takes me a moment to realize that my mother has slapped me.

My mother, who has stolen from me, slapped me.

Her hand, the one that just came in contact with my check, is now covering her mouth. "Oh, Lexi, I'm so . . ." She reaches out to me.

I pull away and run out of the back room and through the store as quickly as I can. So many thoughts are spinning through my head. My money is gone. My mom hit me. I will never get to New York. I will never get out of here.

I realize that I was supposed to meet up with Cam at the mall. But I can't see her right now. I can't see anybody right now. I don't want anybody to know what happened to me. And I can't go back to my house. I have nowhere to go.

"Lexi!" I hear someone calling after me, but I keep running. I can't talk to my mom. In fact, I never want to speak to her again.

By the time I get inside my car, my entire body's shaking. I try to put the key into the ignition, but I know that I'm currently in no condition to drive.

"Lexi?" I hear a tap outside the passenger-side window. "Are you okay?"

I turn to see Logan. The one person I'm supposed to have out of my mind is standing right in front of me with genuine concern etched on his face. He points to the lock. I close my eyes for a few moments, wishing for him to disappear. Of all the times I've wanted him to be near me, this is a time when I want him to be as far away from me as possible. I don't want him to see me like this, to know what my family's like. I need to hold on to some fantasies, as desperate as they are.

"Lexi, please . . ." I hear him call out to me. I stare straight ahead as I unlock the door.

Logan gets in and touches me lightly on the arm. "What's wrong? Is everything okay?" He speaks softly, as if he's afraid of what he may hear.

I can't speak. I can't do anything but cry.

"What . . ." He reaches up to my still-stinging cheek. I instinctually raise my hand to block him. "Give me a second."

He gets out of the car and I see him talking to his mother in the rearview mirror. His mom looks upset as he pats his hand to his cheek.

He knows.

I look away, not wanting to be further humiliated by my mother.

He opens up the driver's door. "I don't think you should drive right now. Let me take you home."

"I can't go home." I hardly recognize the voice that comes out of me, it's so small, so defeated.

He nods. "Okay. I'll take you wherever you want to go."

"I need to go to Houston." The words coming out of my mouth shock me. I need a parent right now. A parent who won't steal from me. One who won't hit me. One who loves me.

Logan's silent for a few moments. "Okay, I'll take you to Houston."

I get out of the car and try to walk past Logan, but he stops me. He takes his fingers and gently cups my chin. He raises my head so I have to look at him. When I finally make eye contact, I see that his eyes are glassy, like he's about to cry.

"Lexi, I'm so sorry for whatever happened." He gives me a small, yet strained smile. "But everything's going to be all right. I'm here for you."

He wraps his arms around me tight. We sit there in the parking lot for a while, with Logan holding me.

And not even that gives me comfort.

21.

Houston, We Have a Problem

I don't speak for the first half hour we're in the car. Every time I open my mouth to say something, a wave of sadness overwhelms me. It takes everything I have to look straight and remember to breathe.

Mercifully, Logan doesn't say anything. He only drives.

I honestly don't even know what there is to say. I don't even know what I'm going to do when I get to Houston. I know that I'll have to face my mother at some point, but part of me feels the desire to just keep going. Not like I haven't thought about running away with Logan before, but never under these circumstances. Plus, I don't want someone to be with me out of pity.

My thoughts are interrupted when I hear Dad's ringtone awaken my phone. I've been ignoring all the calls from my mom, but since Dad has no idea that I'm heading to him, I should probably pick up.

"Lexi!" He doesn't even let me say hello; he sounds panicked. "Oh, princess, your mom told me everything. I'm so sorry. We're all so worried about you, Lexi. Where are you?"

I can hear him breathing rapidly while he awaits my response. "I'm . . . I'm on my way to see you. I can't . . ." I start crying again.

"Okay, Lexi. I'm on my way to our meeting place. You've got a head start on me, so I'll be a little late. You don't have to come all the way to Houston."

"I can't stay there anymore." I try to speak quietly, but desperation and panic seep through my voice.

I hear Dad sigh. "You can't run away from your problems."

"I CAN'T DO THIS ANYMORE!" I scream into the phone. Something in me has snapped. My anger has now shifted to my father, who gets to live in his little bubble existence and doesn't have to deal with the problems that he left behind. The problems (*his children*) that he abandoned. "I know you don't want me with you because of your new girlfriend, but guess what, Dad? I'm your problem, too. Mom *stole* from me, she *hit* me, she took away everything I've been working toward. How do you expect me to live there after what she did? How can anybody expect me to be able to trust her again?"

I hear him take a deep breath. "Princess, calm down."

"Don't call me that. Don't you ever call me that again. I'm not your *princess*. I'm not some trophy you can take down and admire whenever it's convenient to you."

"*Alexis*, please calm down. It's not good for you to be driving when you're this upset."

"*I'm* not driving." I spit out the words at him like it's his fault that Logan has to bear witness to this.

"Well, I don't like hearing you this upset."

"I don't like *being* this upset."

"I'm going to give you the money, prin — Lexi."

"Why are you covering for her?"

"I'm doing what's best for *you*."

"Then why don't you let me come live with you?" My voice cracks at the end.

"It's . . . complicated." I can hear the hesitation in his voice. But I can also hear that there's no changing his mind. "Let's talk about it when I see you."

"No, I want to know right now." I'm sick of playing all these games. I want, for once, for someone to tell me the truth.

"Oh, Lexi . . ."

And with those two words, I shut myself off again. Just like I had to do all those years to get through the pageants, I pull the plug on Human Lexi and revert to Robot Lexi. *Just go through the motions. Keep your head down.*

"Forget it." I speak in an even tone. "I'm not coming."

I hang up on him and shut off my phone.

I turn toward Logan, who's staring straight ahead at the road like his life depends on it. I don't think I've ever seen anybody so uncomfortable in his life . . . well, maybe me on my first date with Taylor.

"Logan, I'm sorry, but can you turn back?"

He steals a quick glance at me. "Of course. I'll get off at the next exit and turn around. I'm . . . I couldn't help but hear, and I'm so sorry. Do you want to come stay with me? I'm sure my mom wouldn't mind."

I shake my head. "I'll be okay."

I close my eyes and try to think about anything else but what's waiting for me back home. Cam's probably mad at me; she has no idea where I am and probably isn't in the mood to hear who I'm currently with. For a split second, I debate going to Benny's house, but he's with Chris. And I can't pretend that they're my family. There are some things that you can't avoid. And it seems like this problem is one of them.

Thirty minutes later, we pull up outside Logan's house and both get out of the car.

He gives me another hug. The thought of seeing him tomorrow is beyond humiliating. "I really can't begin to tell you how much I appreciate your help today." I hear the words come out of my mouth, but I don't feel anything but exhaustion. "And apologize to your mom for me for tearing you away at the last minute. I —"

Logan puts his hand on my shoulder. "It's okay. I'm sorry you had such a rough day. You know you can call me if you need anything."

"Thanks."

Logan hesitates. "Are you sure you don't want to come inside?"

"No. I should really get going." But I don't move, not wanting to go home.

"You're positive?"

No, not at all.

I muster up the best smile I can give him. "Yes, everything's going to be fine."

Even as the words escape my mouth, I know they're not true.

22.

Loathe the One You're With

I pull up outside our house. I don't hesitate for a single second. I feel it's like ripping off a bandage.

I open the front door and head straight to my bedroom.

"Oh, Alexis, I've been worried sick, honey. I'm so —"

I slam my bedroom door shut and block out my mother's apologies. Of course she's sorry, but it doesn't change what happened. It doesn't change what she did.

I ignore her knocking on my door and take off my clothes. I strip away the Lexi who caused all of this.

Not one thing has changed for me.

I put on my robe, open up the door, and come face-to-face with The Momster.

"Sweetie, I can't —"

"Please move aside so I can use the bathroom." I manage to keep my voice monotone, just like a robot. I figure that's the only way I'm going to survive living here for the next year and a half.

"Oh." She moves so I can cross the hallway and get into our bathroom. I turn on the hot water and let steam fill the room so I can no longer see my tear-soaked face, my eyes smudged from all the running mascara. *Waterproof, my foot.*

I stand under the scalding water and close my eyes. I feel at peace and wonder how long I can stay here. Maybe if I stand in the shower long enough, I'll shrivel up and can just float down into the drain. Then I wouldn't have to deal with the world.

Suddenly cold water comes at me and jolts me out of my solitary moment. I quickly shut off the water and dry myself off. I wipe the condensation off the mirror and study my face. I start to take off the remaining makeup and put my hair in a ponytail.

Maybe I should go back to being Boring Lexi. She didn't get into as much trouble as Lexi 2.0.

I head back into my bedroom and ignore Mom's pleas for me to talk to her. Mackenzie must've been sent to her room so she didn't have to witness this. Mom needs to keep her favorite daughter on her side. I blare my music and put on sweats. I turn on my phone and find that I have nine voice mails.

Mom: *Please pick up, Lexi. I'm so sorry. I don't know what came over me, I would never hurt —*

Delete.

Mom: *Where are —*

Delete.

Mom: *Pick up the —*

Delete.

Cam: *Hey. Where are —*

Delete.

Mom: *Lex —*

Delete.

Dad: *I'm on my way to see you, please don't turn around —*

Delete.

Taylor: *Hey there, I —*

Delete.

Cam: *Seriously? You're standing me up? I can't believe —*

Delete.

Dad: *I'm here. Where are you? I'm worried to death, Lexi. Please call me.*

Delete.

I shut off my phone and toss it on the floor. Sleep is the only option I have left, so I throw my blanket over my head and take it.

* * *

There's a knock on my door. I roll over and ignore it.

The door cracks open and Mackenzie pops her head in. "Hey, Lexi, it's almost time for school."

"I'm not going."

She comes and sits on my bed. "Are you sick?"

"Yes." I turn away from her.

She hesitates. "What's going on? Mom and Dad were on the phone all last night. Mom was crying. I'm worried."

I sit up. "Everything's fine. There's nothing for you to worry about. It's just a little disagreement between me and Mom."

It's clear she can see right through my lies. "Does it have to do with me or the pageants?" Her bottom lip juts out, and I can tell that she's about to cry.

"No. It has to do with an issue Mom and I need to work out."

I say it like it's no big deal, but I honestly have no idea how we'll be able to fix something like this.

Mom opens the door. "Mackenzie, go brush your teeth."

Mac gives me a little kiss on the cheek and heads out. I lie back down and pull the blanket over my head.

"Alexis, I really would like to talk to you."

I say nothing.

"Okay, I'll call the school and tell them you aren't coming in today. But when I get back from work, I want us to sit down and talk. I'm very sorry I hit you, honey —"

"You hit Lexi!" I hear Mac's voice cry out. "How could you do that?"

"I told you . . ."

I can't tell if she goes after Mac or if they're both still in my room, but I figure it's best to lie here and play dead.

I flinch slightly when a hand is placed on my back. "I'm leaving, but I mean it. We need to talk. Okay?"

I don't move. I stay there for what seems like a century, until I think it's safe. I slowly pull off the blanket and cautiously walk to the hallway. It appears as if everybody's gone. I walk over to the front window and peek out to see only my car out front. I can't remember the last time I had the house to myself for a day. I turn on the TV and put on a game show. I head over to the refrigerator. The Greek nonfat yogurt and berries that I usually have for breakfast don't seem too appealing. I open up the freezer and grab some of Mac's frozen chocolate chip waffles and stick them in the toaster. I cover them with butter and maple syrup. I'm shoving them in my mouth so fast I hardly taste them.

I don't think I've ever been so hungry in my life. It's like I have this emptiness inside me and the answer is in the kitchen pantry. I plant myself in front of the TV and eat mindlessly. I hardly realize it's almost noon when I'm startled by a knock at the door. I wipe potato chips from my shirt as I get up.

I wasn't really sure who I was going to see, but when I open the door, I'm not very happy to find Taylor standing there.

"Hey. Come here." He grabs me by the waist and gives me a hug.

"You weren't in school and Logan mentioned that he saw you last night. He didn't really say much, just that you had a rough night."

I nod.

He studies my face. "Do you want to talk about it?"

I shake my head.

"Oh, well, I've been texting you and calling you, but I think you shut off your phone." He rocks back and forth on his heels.

I nod again.

"Okay. Um . . ." He studies me up and down. I know I look awful. I went to bed with wet hair that's in something that resembles a ponytail, and dirty, oversized sweats.

He looks around and sees junk food piled up on the coffee table. "I headed out during lunch to check in on you, but I can play hooky for the rest of the day if you want company."

I shake my head . . . yet again.

"So I guess our date tonight is off?" he asks.

I try to smile this time while I nod.

"Okay, you're kind of freaking me out. Are you mad at me?"

I begin to shake my head, but instead say, "No."

"Well, I guess that makes me feel a little better." He gives me a little smile, which quickly fades when I pull away from his outstretched arms. "I don't really know what's going on, and I can't say I'm thrilled I had to find that *something* was going on from Logan."

I just stare at him.

"You gotta give me something to work with here, Lexi." Frustration is seeping into his voice.

I sit down on the couch and Taylor follows me. "I had a pretty major fight with my mom," I say. "I don't really want to get into it. But Logan saw me right afterward and he helped me. It's nothing. I couldn't face school today."

He rubs my back. "Okay. If you want to talk about it sometime, just say the word."

After we sit in silence for about a minute, he gets up. "I guess I should leave you to . . ."

I follow him to the door.

"Yeah, so I guess I'll see you tomorrow. . . ." He leans in and I turn my face. I'm not in the mood for kissing or anything resembling human contact right now. Plus, I didn't have any motivation to brush my teeth this morning.

"Most likely." I don't even want to think about tomorrow. Annoyance flickers across his face for a few seconds before he gives me a weak smile. "Thanks for stopping by, really. I'm just not in a good mood." He doesn't deserve to be treated like this, but I truly don't have the energy to give anybody comfort at this moment.

"Yeah, I guess I can tell that you weren't expecting company." He lets out a little laugh and nods at my outfit.

"You know, this is pretty much what I look like underneath all the makeup and hair product."

He crinkles his brow at me. "Okaaaay."

"Yeah, let's not pretend that you'd be caught dead being seen with me if I always looked like this."

He flinches. "Where did that . . . what are you even talking about?"

I'm so tired. I'm tired of all the lies, all the deception. Might as well finally tell the truth, even if it hurts.

"Oh, come on. You didn't show any interest in me until I started dressing like all those Glamour Girls at school. Don't pretend you care about anything but how I look."

He studies me like I'm an alien life-form. "Lexi, look. I know you're upset, so I'm going to go. I only wanted to make sure you were okay. The last thing I want to do is get into a fight."

"I'm not fighting. I'm simply stating the truth."

He throws his hands up in the air. "I'll talk to you later. Feel better, okay."

"Whatever."

He stands there for a few seconds, looking at me, waiting for something. Then, when I don't give it to him, he finally turns around and heads to his car.

I close the door and head back into the kitchen to see what the freezer has in store for me.

Oh, there's a fresh pint of Chubby Hubby ice cream.

This day has just gotten considerably better. Not like it had much further to fall.

* * *

I think this is what they call a food coma. My stomach's bloated from all the food I've eaten (or, more appropriately, *shoved in my face*).

When I hear the door again, I ignore it. Maybe I should take a nap. Plus, what if it's Logan, or worse, Taylor again?

I know I was a little harsh with Taylor, but I'm sick of pretending that everything is fine with my family and that what he and I have is real. I bet anything that he won't be calling me now that he's seen the *true* me.

There's a knock at the window. "Lexi! Please open up!" It's Benny and Cam.

I have to roll over to get up.

I open up the door and head back to the couch without greeting them.

Benny's eyes are wide as he takes in all the junk food surrounding the area.

I start to uncontrollably sob. "I'm sorry I didn't meet you yesterday, Cam." With everything going on, I can't face the fact that, on top of everything else, I'm a horrible friend.

She kneels down next to me. "Oh, Lexi, you don't need to apologize. I had no idea what was going on. And I never heard from you. Then Benny mentioned he hadn't heard from you, either, and you weren't at school or returning any of the texts we sent you today. We were worried. Then Logan asked me how you were handling everything, and when he realized that I didn't know what he was talking about, he started to walk away. I had to basically block him from the exit and threaten his life for him to tell me what's going on."

A small smile creeps on my face at the thought of tiny Cam intimidating Logan. I could totally see it happen. She does not take the word *no* very well.

"Wait a second." Benny leans in so he's only an inch from my face. "Is that possibly a smile we see?"

I stick my tongue out at him.

"Real mature."

I shrug my shoulders. "I figure being the responsible one has gotten me nowhere, so I'm going to start acting like the spoiled brat my mother apparently thinks I already am."

Cam takes both of my hands. "What happened? I want to hear it from you."

Benny and Cam listen patiently as I recount yesterday's events. Part of me is detached from what I'm saying. Another part, that's growing more and more by the minute, is mad. Mad at myself for sitting here all day and feeling sorry for myself. Mad that I shoved my face full of food that's bad for me. Mad that I'm basically lying down and letting it happen to me.

"ENOUGH!" I shout out, startling Benny and Cam. "Sorry. I've had it. I'm sick of pretending to be someone I'm not. I'm so over my family, but I'm not going to let them push me around."

"So what are you going to do?" Benny asks.

"I have no idea, but I can tell you one thing." I quickly run into my bedroom and grab a few things. "I'm done with this." I hold up a pair of fake eyelashes and drop them into the trash. "And this." One of my

Team Mackenzie T-shirts follows suit. "I'm getting rid of everything fake in my life, including fake people."

I walk over to them. Benny pretends to shield himself. "Don't put me in with the trash, I'll do whatever you want!"

"No, I'd never throw you out."

I wrap my arms around my two best friends. And just like that, a small, yet very important piece of my life snaps back into place.

I don't know why I thought moving to Houston would be a good idea. I couldn't do anything without Benny and Cam. And that realization hits me the most when I hear Mom's car pull up outside.

"Do you want us to leave?" Cam asks as she looks at the door with nervous anticipation.

"No, please stay."

I haven't really thought about dealing with Mom. But I figure she can't do anything with company around. She's all about appearances. At the pageants, she's the smiling mom, always talking sweetly to the other contestants. It isn't until we're behind closed doors that her true thoughts on the competition come out.

Mackenzie opens the door and smiles at us. Mom hesitantly walks in.

"Well, hello, everybody." Mom's clearly taken aback by my visitors. "How are you feeling, Lexi?" She acts like everything's fine. It isn't until she sees the uncomfortable reaction she gets that she realizes that the act is for naught. Nobody here's buying the concerned-mother routine.

"I'm fine," I tell her in my frostiest voice.

"Well . . ." Mom wipes her hands as if she's Lady Macbeth. "Lexi, I think that maybe your friends should leave since you're *not feeling well.*"

As if we need to keep up the facade for Benny and Cam. Like they're going to call up the school and tell the principal that I wasn't sick today after all. At least not the kind of sickness that's contagious. No, what I have could be classified as an infection brought on by the most toxic person in my life.

"I'd prefer that they stay." It's as if I'm willing Mom to have another episode in front of witnesses.

So we all just sit there, not saying a word.

Finally, after a few awkward minutes of this, Cam says, "The two of you need to talk." She turns to Benny. "We should go." Then she turns to me, "But if you want us to come back, call and we'll be back here before you even notice we were gone."

I realize she's right — this is between Mom and me, and as much as I want my friends to be in my corner, there's no way an honest conversation is going to happen if they're in the room.

I get up, and both Cam and Benny give me hugs and whisper encouraging words before they leave.

By the time I turn back around to face Mom, I realize that Mackenzie is in her room. It's only the two of us.

"Please sit down." Mom motions toward the couch. "I wanted to talk to you, Lexi. First, I'm so sorry that I slapped you yesterday. It's unforgivable, and I can understand if you hate me."

I stay silent.

Mom starts wringing her hands. "I also shouldn't have taken the money without your permission. I was in a tight spot with the bills. I maxed out both of my credit cards, and I didn't know what else to do."

I want to say, *Stop throwing so much money away on pageants*, but I think the entire solar system is aware of my feelings on the subject.

"Your father is going to put the money back into your account, and I am going to pay him back. What I did was extremely unfair."

She keeps looking at me like she expects me to pretend that everything is just hunky-dory between us. I can appreciate a nice (perhaps even sincere) apology, but it still doesn't erase the past.

"I talked to work and I'm going to start adding some extra shifts. Inventory is coming up and I can make time and a half. I'll need some help looking after Mackenzie during those days and would appreciate it if you could help out. I already know you do a lot, and can understand if you don't want to."

I realize that this is truly the first time that I've been asked if it's okay for my schedule to revolve around Mackenzie. And to be honest, that little gesture does mean *something* to me. Let's face it, I'm going to have to do it anyway. What's the point of Mom working extra if we have to pay for a babysitter? Mac can pretty much take care of herself, I only need to be around. Pretty much every time I watch her, I stay in my room and do homework while she watches TV. It's an arrangement that works for us both.

If I'm going to live here until college, I should do my best to try to make it as pleasant as possible for us all, including myself.

"I should be able to help out," I say. "For Mackenzie's sake. Not yours."

Mom almost doesn't know how to respond to my positive (albeit somewhat hostile) agreement. "Understood, and I do appreciate it. Do you want to go out to dinner with us? We can go wherever you want."

"That's okay," I say. Her face falls. "I'm not really hungry. I had a lot of junk food today."

It's clear from the look on her face that she doesn't believe me. But just wait until she reaches for her late-night snack of potato chips and dip and finds it gone . . . with the ice cream and cheese sticks and cookies (Oh my!).

I guess I'm more like my mom than I care to admit.

She takes a hesitant step toward me. "So are we are all right?"

"No," I tell her honestly. "Not yet."

I see tears start welling up in her eyes. "I guess that's all I can ask for."

I don't think I can handle much more crying. I get up and head to my room. I have a ton of homework to catch up on.

After all, I need to keep up my grades to get as far away from here as possible.

23.

Hopelessly Devoted to Delusions

I knew I couldn't avoid school another day. Plus, I'm pretty sure it wouldn't be a wise decision to have me around that kitchen unguarded for two days straight. My jeans felt so tight when I zipped them up this morning.

I also knew that I needed to talk to Taylor. I'm not completely surprised to see him waiting for me at my locker.

"Hey," he says quietly.

"Hi."

He rubs my arm. "You feeling better?"

"Yeah. I'm really sorry I was . . . Well, I wasn't myself yesterday and I shouldn't have been so mean."

He nods. "Yeah, it wasn't fun."

The awkwardness between us is so obvious. I'm not exactly sure what to do. I like Taylor, I do. But I can't shake the feeling that he's only interested in me for the wrong reasons.

I'm waiting for him to make a comment on my appearance. I only spent about twenty minutes getting ready this morning. I have my hair up in a high ponytail with a few curls and have on about half the makeup as normal. No more fake eyelashes, no more anything that isn't me.

I've got to find some balance in my life. It doesn't kill me to put in some effort since it makes me feel good about myself. However, I don't want something as superficial as physical appearance to get in the way of being truly happy.

Taylor runs his fingers through his hair. "Listen, I think we need to talk."

I nod. I knew this was coming. If it wasn't my disheveled appearance yesterday, my attitude certainly put a nail in this coffin.

"It's okay, I know what you're going to say. And I understand."

He looks confused. "Understand what?"

"That you're breaking up with me." I can't believe how well I'm handling my first breakup.

"I wasn't going to —"

"Listen, Taylor, no one is blaming you, and I'm not saying it's because of the, um, non-glam look I'm now sporting."

"You're on this again?"

I put up my hands. "Look, I don't want to get into a fight with you. I'm trying to make it easier on you. Seriously. It's okay. We can still be friends." I know people say that a lot when they end a relationship (at least they do in the movies I've seen) and mostly it's only a line, but I really mean it. I want to be friends with Taylor. I want to get to know him better and for him to get to know the real me as well. And who knows, maybe someday, when I'm not a walking mess, we can try it again.

But the look on Taylor's face right now tells me that he isn't seeing it the same way as me. "Oh, and I guess it shouldn't really come as a big surprise that you want to end our relationship right after Alyssa breaks up with Logan?"

"WHAT?"

"Please, like it's some big shock. They've been fighting for months."

They have? Every time I see them together, Logan's always kissing her or putting his hand on her leg or he . . . I mean, I guess it's usually him being affectionate and, honestly, I usually go off into one of my delusional fantasies, so I don't really pay attention to how she reacts.

Taylor shakes his head. "I figure most of the girls here have been biding their time until he was single, but I was hoping you weren't one of them. I guess I was wrong."

"I didn't know —"

"Don't pretend that this isn't why *you* are breaking up with *me*. Well, I guess you have your wish." He turns on his heel and walks away.

Benny comes running over. "What's with Taylor? He seems mad."

"Did Logan and Alyssa break up?"

Benny shakes his head. "I don't know. I haven't heard anything. But come to think of it . . ."

"What? Tell me!"

Benny's obviously proceeding with caution. I'm technically not supposed to be thinking about Logan, and I'm especially not supposed to talk about him since my Loganvention. But after what happened the other day, Benny and Cam realize that I'm going to have to deal with what he saw.

"Nothing, I saw him a few minutes ago and he didn't look so hot. And there was whispering."

Wow. I already feel like I'm walking a tightrope. If this news is true, I'm about to fall. Hard.

It's confirmed. Logan's single. I hear it from Alyssa's best friend, Lisa, first period.

"I'm surprised he didn't see it coming," Lisa says to a crowd of girls that includes me. "I mean, Logan's such a nice guy and they've known each other forever, which made it especially hard for Alyssa to have to break up with him. She loves him, but like a brother, not a boyfriend. It's hard, you know, Logan's always been there for her, and it made it harder and harder for Alyssa to cut the cord. But sometimes you need to make a break, you know. I think Logan could tell, which is why he's been super clingy lately, but his neediness kind of sealed the breakup.

But Alyssa sincerely wants to keep him as a friend, though. I mean, Logan is *such a nice guy*."

Wow. I think being labeled a "nice" guy is the male equivalent of "great personality." Poor Logan. There's nothing wrong with being a nice guy, but I guess if there wasn't a spark it couldn't be forced. And if I think back on it, he has been overly affectionate lately and Alyssa hasn't seemed pleased. I took it more as a reflection of my jealousy, not on the state of their relationship.

My shock over the breakup conflicts with the fact that Logan Reeves is, in fact, now single. But what surprises me the most is that I'm not as happy as I thought I'd be when they broke up. To be honest, I'm relieved that there are so many things for people to gossip about instead of my somewhat-reversion back to a normal-looking person. Nobody really seems to be batting an eyelash that I'm not as glammed up. It's not the response I got when I first came to school looking like a different person. Maybe people don't really care that much about what I look like. Maybe my new look was just a way for people to notice me, and now that they have, I don't need fake hair to be paid attention to.

I feel so bad for Logan — and more awkward thinking about him than ever before. I'm still horrified that he had to witness the crumbling of my family. And now this.

Since I used to revolve my entire school routine around when I was most likely to see him in the hallways, it's just as easy to revolve my routine around avoiding him. I don't see him at all. At least not physically. Mentally is another thing altogether.

I mean, the guy I've been in love with for years is finally single.

For two years I've been telling myself that it's because of Alyssa that he's not with me. But most likely (irony alert!) he's just not into me *that way*. It's easier to blame things on other people, but when you have to look inside and face the facts, it can be ugly.

For two days I manage to avoid Logan. But I know it'll only be a matter of time before my luck runs out.

I see Logan coming down the hallway at the end of the day. He usually takes a different route to his locker, so he's surprised me. He sees me and waves frantically. I keep looking around the hallway like I'm a little kid seeing tall buildings for the first time.

He finally catches up. "Hey." He looks me in the eye. "Are you avoiding me?"

I give him a *who-me?* look. "What?"

He seems slightly out of breath. "I've been trying to see you for days now to make sure you're okay. But you're never around and you haven't been answering my texts."

More like I'm always a step ahead of him.

"No, I've been, ah, busy. Um, sorry about you and Alyssa."

That's it. Distract him. Bring up his pain so we don't have to relive yours.

"Thanks. How are things at home?"

It seems like he isn't distracted so easily.

"It's fine. I . . ."

Logan can clearly sense my discomfort. "Do you want to go grab a coffee or something?"

And there it is.

Logan's asking me out for coffee. I've dreamed about him asking me to do anything. Granted, he probably wants to make sure he doesn't have to put me on some sort of depression watch.

But the weird thing is, I'm not even excited. Maybe because I know he's just looking out for his "friend" Lexi. Maybe he'll even ask me for advice on getting Alyssa back. I don't think I have the strength for that.

Luckily, I only have an hour before work. By the time we get to the mall, we'll only have maybe thirty minutes to chat.

For the first time ever, the very last person I want to spend any time with is Logan Reeves.

I never thought it was possible for two human beings to be this uncomfortable around each other.

I'm refusing to make eye contact with Logan. I'm afraid if I do, I'll see that look of pity I so despise. I spent the entire time in line at the coffeehouse staring at the board, even though I knew exactly what I was going to get. Then I nearly knocked over his drink when I reached for mine.

"So . . ." he says to me as we sit down, "how are things at home?"

"Fine." I stare at my peppermint tea like there are secret messages in the steam coming from the cup. "How are things with you?"

"Fine."

Silence. Awkward, painful *why-did-I-agree-to-this?* silence.

"Is everything okay with your mom?" he asks.

"I guess." I still can't believe he knows what happened. I have to change the topic. Let's see, Logan and I usually talk about pageants or Alyssa, so I'm not really sure what else to talk about. So I reach. "How's the football team going to be next year?"

"Awesome!" he answers enthusiastically. "I really think that Taylor, oh . . ."

So apparently there's no other subject we can talk about. We have nothing else in common. How is that possible?

"You know what's funny?" he asks.

That we have absolutely nothing to talk about?

I decide to say "What?" instead.

"I think this is the first time we've both been single."

"Uh-huh." How do I remind him that with the exception of the past few weeks, I have always been single, while he has always had a girl-friend of Alyssa-like stature (read: gorgeous)? And until Alyssa, he's always been the one to do the dumping.

"You know what?"

"What?" Man, this is kind of annoying. If he wants to say something to me, why doesn't he just say it? Even though he's right across from me, all I can think about is how I'd rather be with Taylor. Even though when I *was* with Taylor, all I could think about was Logan.

If only Benny and Cam had thought of the Loganvention sooner.

"I don't know . . . Maybe . . ." I finally look at him and see that he's blushing. I quickly scan the coffee house to see if anybody we know has walked in. "Hey, do you want to go to the athletic dinner with me? I mean, I'm not really ready to jump into dating, and I think it would be fun for us to go together. You know, as friends."

Yes, *friends*. Friend Lexi's back. Because no matter what I do to change me, I can't really change the way someone feels about me. No amount of primping in the world can make Logan feel the way for me that I have for him.

The truth does hurt, but I think maybe it's time that I bring myself back to reality. Logan will never see me that way.

Or.

I can finally go out with Logan. A lot of things have changed, but one thing hasn't. Logan Reeves is literally the man of my dreams.

So of course I say yes.

But as soon as I say yes, I can't help but wonder what will happen when fantasy and reality finally collide.

24.

Playing with the Queen of Snark

I come home late from work to find Mom sitting in the living room, waiting for me. Things continue to be strained between us, so we both try to stay out of each other's way. I do truly believe she's sorry, but one apology isn't going to erase the past few years.

"How was your day?" she asks.

"Fine." It's funny, because I always imagined that when Logan finally asked me to do something, I'd be dancing around as if my life had suddenly become a musical. Or there'd be forest animals following me around, celebrating my joy.

Reality, it seems, has not been as kind to me.

"So . . ." I can tell by her strained smile that she needs something from me. "We have inventory next weekend, and I'd really like to pull a late-night double shift to get some more money."

I'm appreciative that I'm being asked first, but then I remember that next weekend is the athletic dinner . . . and Mackenzie's Little Miss Dallas pageant.

Perfect.

"I was wondering if you could take Mackenzie to her pageant on Saturday morning. It's only thirty minutes away and I'll be able to get there by the start of the pageant itself. I just need you to take her there and help her get ready. I'd really appreciate it. *We'd* really appreciate it."

"I got invited to go to the booster's athletic dinner and dance that Friday night."

Mom nods. I'm sure she assumes it's with Taylor. I haven't told her we broke up. I haven't really told her much of anything lately. "Is there a reason you can't do both? I'll have Mac stay over at a friend's and I'll even lift your curfew on Friday night. You have to be at the pageant no later than seven in the morning."

No curfew? And I'll be with Logan?

Maybe things are starting to look up after all.

I was too exhausted last night to tell Benny and Cam about Logan. Plus, I knew they wouldn't approve. It was bad enough telling them my version of what happened with Taylor. But since I see both of them waiting for me at my locker this morning, it's obvious that the word has spread.

"Well, good morning, sunshine." Benny gives me a little smirk. "What's up?"

"How did you hear?"

Benny laughs. "I think the more appropriate question would be who *didn't* we hear it from? Even Chris heard, and he's, like, four degrees of separation from Logan."

"I'm sorry." It seems that all I've been doing lately is apologizing to my best friends. "I know I shouldn't be going with him. I do. I know that this might cause me to completely go off the rails, but I . . ."

I stop myself. I don't need to give Cam and Benny a reason for saying yes. We all know that I could've been scheduled for a life-saving operation and I'd have moved it if Logan came calling.

"And you know," I say, almost to remind myself, "we're going as *friends*. Logan said the word *friend* about a gazillion times when he asked me. His intentions were loud and clear." *And a little painful.* But true.

"It's okay," Cam reassures me. "I think you should go. You need to experience this for yourself, and then you'll see it isn't as fun as you think it'll be."

"Thanks." While I'm grateful that she's being supportive (in her own twisted way), the realization that I'm going to the athletic dinner with Logan is starting to sink in.

Cam goes on. "Just let me make something clear; you are so going to owe me. Because I'm not going to let you go alone."

Cam turns around and starts to walk down the hallway . . . right to Grant. She tilts her head and gets his attention easily.

"Oh my God." Benny leans in. "Is Cam *flirting* with Grant?" He looks over at the outside window.

"What are you doing?" I ask.

"Checking to see if it's raining frogs."

We both are blatantly staring at Cam and Grant. Neither of us ever thought we'd see this day happen.

Yes, we've seen a lot of insane things this semester. But this one definitely takes the crazy up a notch.

I've heard of people taking bullets, but Cam has taken a grenade for me. More specifically, a grenade in the shape of a very egotistical, very "handsy" quarterback.

Cam's going to the athletic dinner with Grant. She basically invited herself, and he was powerless to resist.

I'm going to need the strength in numbers, because there are still some people who don't think I should be going at all.

"And here I thought we didn't let just anybody come to the booster dance." I overhear Brooke say to Hannah on my way to lunch.

I decide to do what's best for both of us and ignore her.

That may be easier said than done, since I can't help but notice who Brooke sits right next to at the Beautiful People table and wraps her bony arm around. Who she leans into as she whispers in his ear.

Taylor.

"Lexi?"

I turn around to see Hannah looking at me with concern.

"Is everything all right?" she asks quietly.

I can't tell if she's out to get intel for Brooke or if she's genuinely worried. I'm not sure if my little outburst at SuperStore made its way up to the corporate office. Or if she's also noticing Brooke practically shoving her tongue in Taylor's ear.

"I'm fine," I reply.

"Oh, okay." She pauses before she heads to the table. "It's just that you haven't seemed like yourself lately."

But oddly enough, this is the most I've felt like myself in a really long time.

25.

Reality Bites

I've been staring at my mascara wand for nearly ten minutes. It's the athletic dinner, so I know I should try to look extra nice. I mean, I guess having Logan picking me up in an hour does put a little more pressure on me, but I don't want to think tonight is anything but a simple matter of me being a plus one. It's only a number, it's not a date.

"Oh, for the love!" Cam comes into the bathroom and yanks the wand from my hand. "Are you still fretting over how much makeup to wear? It's okay to want to look nice. Just cool it on the hairspray since I'm convinced that's what made you go a little nuts." She winks at me as she goes back into my bedroom.

I couldn't agree more. On both parts.

I put the finishing touches on my outfit. I've dreamed of something like this happening for so long and now I'm not even that excited. More nervous than anything.

I grab my purse and meet Cam in the living room.

"I'm trying to figure out something." Cam looks around the empty house. "Do you think your mom is the most trusting mother in the world for letting you have the house to yourself tonight, or is she in denial about what happens after the athletic dinner?"

"Most likely, she doesn't think I have it in me."

Cam smirks at me. "Do you?"

"Yeah, like I really want people to see where I live. Heaven forbid anything happened to Mac's shrine."

She comes over and takes my hands. "Turn around — I want a look at you."

I try not to groan as I model for Cam.

"You really look beautiful, Lexi. But I always thought that. I'm glad that you're starting to see yourself as more than a 'Great Girl' for a change."

"Thanks." I run my hand down my little black dress. "You look amazing, too."

"What? This old thing." Cam spins so her red dress flies slightly open to reveal a little leg. We take a few pictures and text them to Benny and Chris, who are having their own "anti-athletic dinner" with some friends over at Benny's. They plan on doing as little athletic activity as possible, and instead of celebrating egos, they're feting sloth and gluttony.

Cam takes another look at her dress. "I hope Grant doesn't get any ideas. I forgot my Mace."

"Maybe we should bring a water sprayer. I hear that works on dogs."

"Man-sized ones?" she asks.

"We could always try it out."

Cam looks thoughtful for a moment, but then we hear the doorbell ring.

"You should get it," she whispers.

I take a deep breath and go over to open up the door.

How many times have I dreamed of this moment?

Logan's standing outside our door with a black suit on . . . and roses.

He brought me roses.

I open up the screen door and Cam quickly pops out to meet Grant, who's peeking over Logan's shoulder.

"Hi." I try to remain calm.

"Hey, you look beautiful." He hands me the roses.

"Thanks." I stare at him, not sure what to do next. Sure, I've dreamed of this scenario so many times. This would be the part when he usually confesses his love to me, we start making out, and, well, I really must censor the next part. It's, *ahem*, private.

I guess I never considered that this could be a reality. That we'd have to do the small talk and everything else that people do on a first date. Although this is clearly *not* a first date.

I have a feeling that I'm going to need to remind myself of that a lot this evening. *A lot.*

"I should put these in water." This is the first time I've ever gotten flowers from someone who isn't my dad. I run into the kitchen to find a vase, but we really don't have a lot of need for vases in this house. Instead I decide to use one of those Big Gulp plastic cups, since it's big enough to hold a dozen roses.

When I enter the living room, Logan's studying the mantel filled with photos of Mackenzie's various pageants. I see him flinch slightly when he comes across one that has Alyssa in it.

"I guess we should go. . . ."

He looks up at me. "Sounds good." He holds open the door for me and places his hand on the small of my back. I keep my eyes straight forward and will myself to the car. Every ounce of strength I have is focused on getting to the car because if I don't, I may tackle Logan to the ground.

Thank God Cam's here. She's probably the only person who could subdue me. Forget the fact that the entire football team will be there — petite Cam is the only one with the courage to take me down if need be.

I've got to admit, this dance is kind of boring. Usually Benny and I would keep Cam company as she got ready, and then he and I would watch movies and order pizza. I always imagined that I was missing something, that my adolescence wouldn't be complete without partaking in the high school ritual of attending dances or the infamous athletic dinner.

The dinner itself wasn't very memorable. It was filled with a lot of grandstanding, boring speeches, something that I think was supposed to be chicken, and a bunch of inside jokes (either that or I lost my sense of humor on the drive over). I'm grateful that we weren't at the same table as Taylor and his date, Brooke.

After the tables were cleared, the dance floor opened, but nobody's even dancing. The guys are all in a group talking about whatever it is that guys talk about, while Cam and I are avoiding the Glamazon Girls.

"So this is it?" I look hopefully at Cam, willing her to tell me that in a few minutes the magic will start and we'll all be dancing and laughing together like lifelong friends.

She shrugs. "The guys will start dancing once the DJ starts playing some annoying hip-hop song. They'll all dance around like they're hotshots, when in fact, they'll look like a bunch of tools. But —"

Hopes up!

"I've seen some of the guys sneaking swigs out of a flask that Grant brought, so they'll probably start feeling frisky during the next round of cheesy ballads."

Nice!

Cam obviously sees how excited this gets me. "At what point is it okay to smack you?"

"What?"

She shakes her head. "Honestly, Lex, I thought you already saw that being with that group isn't as exciting as you thought it would be. And being with Logan won't make it any better. At least I thought you understood that when you were with Taylor." Cam moves her chin slightly in the direction past my left shoulder.

I discretely turn around and find Taylor standing there with Brooke draped around him.

She continues. "You know, I always lumped all those jocks into one group. And you're well aware that I've questioned Taylor's intentions with you, but even I have to admit that Taylor treated you well. I think he's in a completely different league than Logan."

"Blasphemy!" I shout at her. But truthfully, I never really felt like an outsider when I was with Taylor. He went out of his way to make me feel comfortable. I can't help but think how different this evening would be if Taylor and I were still together. But we aren't. He's with Brooke. And I'm with Logan.

Cam and I spend the next half hour near the dessert table, taste-testing the various cookies on display. We're having an epic debate between peanut butter oatmeal and classic chocolate chip when a slow song starts playing.

I look up and find Logan's eyes locked on mine. He starts walking over to me and I grab Cam's elbow.

"Oh Lord." I hear her say under her breath. "I'm heading to the bathroom for Grant's safety."

Logan smiles at me. "It's a dance. I figure we should dance."

I nod and he takes my hand. We walk to the dance floor and he turns to me. He wraps his arms around me and holds me close. I nuzzle slightly into him and I see goose bumps pop up on the back of his neck.

Did *I* do that?

If so, *awe*-some.

"You know . . ." He pulls us apart slightly so our faces are only a couple inches away. "I always wanted you to come to these dances so we'd have a chance to dance together. But I'm glad you didn't come until now. I don't think I could've handled seeing you with anybody else."

He pulls me back to him and his grasp tightens around me.

Remember to breathe, Lexi. I really hope that I'm not hallucinating any of this. Since I'm pretty sure I've dreamed of him saying something like that to me before. But it was a little different. I guess, for one, it was a dream and this is (*oh please, oh please*) reality. But in my dreams, when Logan pulled me close and held on to me, I didn't smell alcohol on his breath.

But hey, nobody's perfect.

The after-party is at Josh's house. Yes, I finally make it to one of Josh's infamous parties. His parents are extremely wealthy and have a tendency to turn a blind eye to their only son's, shall we say, social events.

By the time we get there, most of the Glamour Girls are in the pool.

Funny, it never crossed my mind that I needed to bring a (skimpy) bikini to an after-party. How foolish of me. Such a rookie move on my part. My bad.

Logan and crew immediately head to the drinks.

"How much longer is my punishment?" Cam whispers in my ear.

Guilt floods over me. Poor Cam has already had to endure Grant's constant wandering hands and now we're at a party that looks about as fun as another one of Mackenzie's pageants.

In fact, this party reminds me so much of Mac's pageants, especially with everybody parading around in their best evening wear so they can be judged by people who feel like they're better than everybody else. And lets face it — I've been the biggest pageant contestant these past few weeks. I know it was Benny who put me up to it, but it was me who wanted the approval of the Beautiful People for years. And for what?

I can say one thing for certain, it did *not* help with my self-esteem.

I squeeze Cam's hand. "I'm sorry. We can go."

She squeezes back. "No, it's okay. I'm only teasing. I know how long you've been looking forward to this, and I want to be here for you."

"You know I don't deserve you."

"Duh." She bangs her hip against mine.

I look around for Logan, but all I see are the Beautiful People strutting around with their holier-than-thou attitude.

What am I doing here?

Oh, yeah, Logan, who's nowhere to be found.

"I'm going to do another loop to find Logan, and then we can leave."

I start in the kitchen and see the line of people for drinks. Josh's parents did take everybody's keys when they came in and are apparently going to shuttle anybody who isn't fit to drive. How responsible of them.

I go over to the game room, where I see a bunch of guys, including Taylor, playing a football game on the TV. *Single-minded much, fellas?*

Taylor sees me standing there and excuses himself from the game. "Hey." He gives me a quick hug. "You look great."

"Thanks." I look around to make sure Brooke isn't nearby. "Taylor, I want you to know that I'm really sorry about everything." I hesitate, unsure if it's really appropriate for me to be having this conversation with him when we're both here with other people. "I really did like you. But I think I was pretending to be someone I'm not, and I guess I didn't really know where the line was with you, if that makes sense. And I wanted to apologize because I don't think I was very fair to you."

He studies me for a moment.

"I think you should know something." He leans in. "Do you want to know the second I realized I wanted to ask you out?"

I'm pretty sure I do.

"It was when I came into The Cellar and you were so cute and funny bossing me around. I hate shopping, but that night was fun because I was with you. We had never really hung out much before, and I felt that you were someone I wanted to get to know."

I'm speechless. Taylor liked me *because* of my personality?

"Yes, I'd be an idiot if I didn't notice when you started wearing dresses and stuff. But it was the confidence it gave you that made you completely irresistible. But maybe it wasn't confidence if you truly thought that was the only reason I wanted to be with you."

I didn't think it was possible for me to be an even bigger fool, but I was wrong. I was wrong about so many things.

"I didn't . . ." I manage to stammer out. "I thought . . ."

"I guess it doesn't really matter." He gestures over my shoulder. "It looks like you got what you wanted."

Did I?

Taylor walks away and I'm more confused than ever.

"Hey!" I hear Logan's voice behind me. "I've been looking everywhere for you." He puts his arm around me. "No, seriously, I've been looking *everywhere.*"

I'm not sure if I should believe him, since I pretty much haven't left the living room the entire evening. Presumably if someone is looking "everywhere" for you, the main room of the house should be included. But really, I'm just splitting hairs at this point.

"I've got something I want to show you." He leads me past the living room — I shrug in response to Cam's inquiring look — and then takes me upstairs to the second floor. He opens up a random door and leads me into what appears to be a spare bedroom.

My heart starts racing. What, exactly, does Logan want to show me?

He gives me a crooked smile. "Alone at last."

He sways slightly, and then grabs me by the waist.

"Hey," he says.

"Hey," I reply, not knowing what else to say, or what's going on.

"Hey," he whispers earnestly in my ear.

Please do not tell me this is Logan's way of flirting. It'd be such a disappointment.

He studies me for a few seconds and then moves his hands up and down my arm. "Oh, Lexi . . . I just can't . . ."

I can't tell if he's drunk or flustered.

Or maybe a little of both.

He begins to shake his head back and forth. "Oh man, I never thought we'd get here. You know?"

Tell me about it.

"You . . ." He steps away and smiles as he looks me up and down. "You're certainly full of surprises."

Yeah, it seems like I'm not the only one.

"Do you have any idea how hard it was for me to keep my hands off of you when you came to school that day with the" — he gestures at my legs — "on."

Is he talking about the first day I wore a dress? Because I'm pretty sure I always have my legs on.

He starts laughing. I can smell the alcohol on his breath. I close my eyes for a second, trying to collect my thoughts.

"You're so amazing, Lexi. You're, like, the coolest girl, and, like, we get along so well and stuff, and now you're, like, hot all of a sudden."

I try to smile at him. They say that alcohol can bring out the truth, so maybe it's time I get to find out what Logan really thinks. To stop making up these fairy tales in my mind that he's my Prince Charming.

Last time I checked, I'm pretty sure Prince Charming didn't require a bottle of vodka to sweep his princess off her feet.

"It's, like . . ." He bumps into the nightstand and nearly knocks over the lamp. In a flash, Logan's right next to me. He puts his hand around the back of my neck. "I've wanted to do this for so long."

And then Logan kisses me.

Logan Reeves is kissing me.

It's amazing what happens when your dreams come true. Instead of hearing music swell or seeing fireworks go off, the only sensation that's overtaking me is the taste of cigarette smoke and alcohol that's currently being shoved in my mouth.

I try to go out of my body. I refuse to acknowledge this, um, whatever he's doing now (I wonder if he knows that's my nose), as my first kiss with Logan.

It wouldn't be right.

He finally parts from me and he's got a huge grin on his face.

"Hey."

I smile tightly, hoping that he sees it as neither disappointment over what just happened nor an invitation for more.

"Mmmm . . ." He comes back at me, but not for a kiss this time. His face is in my hair and he's taking deep breaths. "Mmmm . . . you're so hot."

He starts kissing my neck, and then my ear. *Oh, please have him realize soon that's my ear.*

"Hey," he whispers again. "You want to know what I think?"

For the first time ever, I have no desire to hear what Logan thinks. Unless it's *I think I should go sober up.*

"I think" — he plays with the strap on my dress — "that you and me . . ."

Logan stops cold. I notice a bead of sweat running down his forehead.

He starts to turn white. "I think . . ."

He grabs his stomach. My instincts kick in and I jump away from him.

"Oh God . . ." He runs for the bathroom and less than two seconds later I hear the über-romantic and oh-so-sexy sound of Logan retching.

I plug my ears in fear that I'll start puking, too, although all I've had to drink tonight is water. I didn't trust anything in the kitchen except for good ol' reliable American tap.

I'm frozen about what to do. What I *want* to do is run out of here and pretend like the last fifteen minutes didn't happen. But I guess I really should make sure Logan's okay.

I take tiny steps toward the bathroom. I pause every time I hear him throw up all over the toilet (not to mention my dreams).

Even though the door's open, I give a little knock.

"Hey." Oh great, *I'm* doing it now. "Ah, do you want me to get you anything?"

I'm afraid to do it, but I look down and see Logan hugging the toilet like it's his best friend. And at this moment, it probably is.

"Do you want me to get anybody?" . . . *to free me from this scenario.*

He shakes his head.

After a few moments, he leans back and studies me for a second. He then gives a little laugh. "Dude, I *so* do not feel good."

Yeah, he's not the only one.

Once Logan's safely passed out on the bathroom floor, I make a break for freedom.

A flash welcomes me when I open the door. After my temporary blindness wears off, I realize that Brooke's standing there with Hannah and Taylor, her camera phone pointed at me.

"I thought we should document this moment. I figure this is your first time, since I can't imagine anybody would want to touch you sober." She has a self-satisfied grin on her face. It's really the first time I realize that Brooke is ugly. Sure, she's pretty to look at, but no amount of primping can hide an ugly person. And that's what she is. Ugly on the inside.

For the past few years, I've kept my comments to myself when it comes to Brooke and her ilk. I've stayed silent. In the process, I've done nothing but torture myself. And for what? To have nights like this? *No, thank you.*

Real Lexi is not going to let Brooke treat her like a second-class citizen anymore.

"So am I a slut or a prude?" I ask her. "You really need to make up your mind — it'd really help me with my college applications."

She laughs at me. I ignore the fact that she's with my somewhat ex-boyfriend, so decide against the easy sloppy seconds comment.

"Logan's really sick," I say to an incredibly uncomfortable Taylor. "He's in the bathroom."

Brooke blocks him from checking it out. "Oh, sure," she says, "*those* were the noises we were hearing." I hear a few more laughs and turn to see that a crowd has gathered at the bottom of the stairs.

"Look, Brooke, I don't know what kind of wild sex you're having that sounds like someone projectile vomiting, but what you do in your free time is really your business. I really couldn't care less about anything you do." I push her aside so I can go down the stairs and get as far away from this party as possible. I'm so tired trying to fit in with them. Why would anybody want to live like this?

"Yeah, like you haven't tried *to be me* these last few weeks," she calls after me.

I hear some "oohs" in the crowd. I catch Cam's eyes and she gives me a supportive nod.

"You know what, Brooke. You're right." Her mouth drops open slightly, surprised at my confession. I turn toward the crowd. "I have tried to be like you guys, to be *liked* by you. And say what you want, but I did it. You all didn't have time for a loser like me unless I was entertaining you or doing something for you. But then I put on some makeup and became one of you. So I guess deep down, we're all losers who have something we want to cover up. Like an eating disorder." I shoot a glance at Brooke. "Or a parent that neglects you.

"We're all the same. So you're not better than me, Brooke. You just like to pretend that you are. Why? To make you feel better about yourself. You know what that makes you? A bully. And in my opinion, bullies are the worst kind of people. Because the people who feel the need to bring others down to feel good about themselves are the ones who need help. And not the help that can be found in the beauty product aisle.

"So I can take off the makeup, but I'm still a good person." I'm now only a couple inches from Brooke's face. "But there's no such thing as bitch remover."

I walk quickly downstairs and push my way to the front door.

Josh's mom's eyes are wide as she opens up the front door for Cam and me. "Lovely party," I say. "You must be so proud."

26.

Take This Crown and Shove It

I'm shocked awake by my alarm clock after only a few hours of sleep, and the entire evening starts flooding back to me. There was always a part of me that knew that if Logan and I were ever to get together, it wouldn't be exactly like I always hoped.

However, I never thought it would be the exact opposite.

As far as I'm concerned, the only bright spot of the evening was telling Brooke off to her face. Although I sincerely doubt that any of what I said got through to her. Despite recent behavior, I can recognize a lost cause.

I try my best to push it all aside and focus on getting Mackenzie to her pageant. I pull up in front of Mac's friend's house and she's already waiting for me outside. I glance at the clock; I'm three minutes late. Hopefully this won't set her off.

"Hi." She gives me a smile and hands me a list Mom gave her to make sure I had everything she needs for today.

I take inventory of the trunk and backseat; all costumes, hairpieces, sugar fixes, etc., are accounted for.

"How was the dance?" Mac asks as she buckles up.

"It was fine." I'm grateful that I don't have to deal with Mom this morning. I'm sure she'd have a lot more questions. "Ready for the pageant?"

She shrugs.

I'd thought Mac would be more excited for the state pageant. If she wins here, she qualifies for Mini Miss Texas, or something like that.

"Actually . . ." Mac starts to fiddle with her newly French manicured fingernails. "Anne and a few other friends are going swimming today, and I wish I could go with them instead."

"Well, there's only one Little Miss Dallas pageant." *Yikes.* Who do I sound like?

"I guess." She starts to sulk and I'm in no mood for it today. Not like I've ever been in the mood for it, but today is not the day to start anything with me.

"You know, Mac, we all put a lot of work and effort into taking you to these pageants. It would be nice if you didn't complain about it constantly."

She doesn't say anything for a few seconds, so I think that maybe I talked some sense into her.

"Lexi, what if I told you I don't want to do pageants anymore?"

I quickly glance at her to see if she's trying to pull something over on me. She looks sad.

"Well, do you?" I ask.

"No. I don't like them. I don't know if I ever did. It's just something Mom and I would do together, and they make her happy. When she asks me if I want to do them, I say yes because I'm afraid of letting her down."

My mind starts to race through different memories of the pageants. Mackenzie did spend a lot of time complaining, but she seemed happy. But that was usually when Mom was happy.

Mac starts quietly crying.

"Mackenzie?" I ask quietly.

"I don't want Mom to hate me."

"Mom won't . . ." I pull the car into a shopping center parking lot. I turn off the engine and spin toward her. "Mackenzie, do you still want to do pageants?"

"No." She starts sobbing.

"You don't have to do them anymore. We can talk to Mom."

She shakes her head fiercely back and forth. "She'll be mad."

"Well, she'll get over it." I don't doubt that Mom will be furious. "Have you told her how you feel?"

Mac nods. "But she doesn't listen."

Tell me about it.

"Lexi?" Mac opens up her bag and hands me a photo. It's of me when I was her age. I've got a yellow sundress on, my hair in two braids, and I'm giving the camera a big, goofy smile. I'm holding someone's (probably Dad's) hand off-camera. "Were you happy when you were my age?"

"Yeah. Being seven's awesome, Mac. You work way too hard. You need to have more fun and play with your friends."

"I don't have a lot of friends, not good friends like you have. And most of the friends I do have make fun of me for being in pageants. All the boys in class call me Miss Ugly America."

"Well, boys are stupid." This makes her laugh. "And the other people who say that aren't really your friends."

Mac takes the picture back and studies it. "Were you happy because I wasn't born yet?"

"Oh God, Mackenzie, don't ever think that. Was I a little upset to have to start changing diapers and be a babysitter? Yeah, maybe. And, well, I know we sometimes have our issues. . . ."

I start to think about my attitude from Mac's point of view. I can see how she thinks I hate her. I mean, it's not like she's been completely innocent in all of this, but she's just a kid, after all.

"We argue, but we're sisters. That's a bond that nobody can ever break, even crazy pageant moms."

I don't blame Mac for being scared of telling Mom. I speak slowly and carefully so Mac absorbs every word. "She has to respect your decision, and we can tell her together."

"But it's our thing."

"Well, you guys can get another thing. Like, I don't know, walking or reading, or, um, other stuff." Mom and I haven't had a normal relationship in years, so I have no idea what mothers and daughters are supposed to do together. "You can't keep doing it just because it's what Mom wants."

"But you have Dad."

"So do you."

Fresh tears start trickling down her face. "Not like you."

"You've been so preoccupied with pageants, Mac. You'll get there. We'll spend more time with him on weekends."

It's true, Mac and Dad have a slightly estranged relationship. He doesn't have any clue how to handle Pageant Mackenzie. I think he's still emotionally scarred from attending one of her pageants years ago at Mom's insistence. He was horrified at the transformation of his then four-year-old daughter into the equivalent of a living doll. He thought it "took away her innocence." I can blame my dad for many things, but I can't blame him for that.

"Yeah, but if I stop doing pageants, what will Mom have?"

I'm speechless. That's too big of a burden for any child to have, especially one so young.

"Oh, Mac, you don't need to worry about that."

"But she only cares about me when I'm on stage."

"That's not true."

Poor Mac. What must it be like to think that neither of your parents cares about you? I spent the first ten years of my life relatively happy, and look at the bitter person I ended up being. What hope does Mac have at happiness if this isn't fixed now?

"Listen, we'll figure something out. I promise you this: You won't have to do pageants anymore. And we'll find out a way to make Mom listen."

"But it's the stage she cares about. That's it."

"Well . . ." An idea flashes in my head. Maybe Brooke isn't the only person who's going to hear me finally tell the truth.

I turn on the ignition. "Buckle up, Mackenzie. We're in for a wild ride."

Miss Lauren's waiting for us when we arrive. "Hey, y'all!" She greets us both with a big hug. "Miss Mackenzie, are you ready for your hair and makeup?"

Mac and I exchange looks.

"Uh-oh." Lauren laughs. "Why do I sense trouble?"

"Hey, Lauren, you remember that big, like *big* hair they had in the eighties with, like . . ." I take my long bangs and stick them straight up.

She eyes me suspiciously. "I'm aware of that decade."

"Do you think you can make my hair look even worse than that? And do you have any fluorescent makeup? I'm thinking neon pink for my eyes."

"Wait, I'm doing *your* makeup?" She looks between Mackenzie and me, wondering what's going on.

Mac jumps up and down. "We're taking a stand!"

"A what?"

I keep my voice low. "I know that the pageant world's important to you, so I don't want you to do anything that'll get you in trouble, but . . ." I quickly look around me so nobody can overhear. "We have a plan and we need your help. I need you to make me up, but not as a pretty beauty queen, but picture a beauty queen from a Stephen King novel and you're halfway there."

To be honest, a small part of me is hoping that she'll object.

But after a few seconds, she nods her head and begins.

It's on.

27.

Judgment Day

Wow.

Just wow.

Mackenzie has spent the last half hour rolling on the floor laughing.

Miss Lauren inspects her creation. "I think it would be best that you don't mention that I did this. I don't think I'd ever work again."

"It'll be our little secret."

There's a knock on the door.

Mac lets our other accomplices in. "We have —" Cam stops dead in her tracks when she sees me.

"It's okay. You can laugh."

Benny's mouth is hanging open. He starts to take me in. "Are you seriously going to go through with this?"

"Yep."

Cam nods approvingly. "Brilliant."

"Here." Benny hands me my sewing machine while Cam puts the garment bags on the bed. He continues to study me. "I'm sorry, I didn't realize that you were planning on auditioning as an Oompa Loompa today."

We may have gone a little overboard with the bronzer on my face. I'm about forty shades darker than my natural skin tone.

Mac hands me three of her old dresses that were in the garment bag.

"Thanks, guys, I really appreciate it."

"It was nothing." Benny can't take his eyes off my face. "And I really mean it was nothing. It's surprisingly easy to break into your house. A key under the welcome mat? Pretty predictable."

"Yeah, but who would want to break into our crap house?"

"Hey!" Mackenzie stands up to me. "That's our home. It isn't great, but it's ours."

I guess she's right. Maybe I need to stop focusing on the family I lost, but finally embrace the family that I have.

Flaws and all.

Although if I'm willing to embrace things that I don't like, I think it's only fair that Mom does, too.

Miss Lauren puts the finishing touches on my eyes. "Okay, I think that's it." She steps back and looks me up and down. She begins to shake her head. "Hon, I understand why you're doing this, but please keep in mind that some of these girls are here on their own accord. True, some people take it too far and I've seen it tear families apart. But please know when you're up there that the pageant circuit does some good." She then bursts out laughing. "I don't know why I'm trying to talk any sense into someone who looks like . . ." She stops herself and walks out the door.

Probably for the best. I'm aware of what I look like and what I'm about to do.

I look at the clock. I have less than forty-five minutes to get this outfit ready. I grab one of Mackenzie's pink beauty dresses. I look at her. "Are you sure you want me to do this?"

She doesn't hesitate for a second. "Yes. Do it."

I tear the dress at the seam. I quickly divide the ruffled skirts and beaded tops from the three dresses. I ignore the fact it only takes minutes to destroy the hours of work it took to get these dresses perfect for Mackenzie.

I lay out my blue one-piece swimsuit and put together the deconstructed dresses like they're pieces of a puzzle. My fingers work quickly, rearranging and sewing. I have to push my perfectionist tendencies aside as I work on this. I'm aware that the colors (hot pink, dark blue, and bright yellow) don't go together. My seams are crooked; you can see the stitches holding together the beading work. But perfection isn't the point. It's pretty much the opposite of what we're trying to accomplish today.

243

There are only a few minutes left before we have to head down for the lineup. I put the half-finished ensemble on and instruct Benny and Cam to pin, sew, and even glue the remaining pieces together.

Once they finish, they both stand back and look at me, and it's clear they're trying hard not to laugh.

Benny takes out his cell phone. "I'm sorry, but I so need to send Chris a photo of this. There's no way he's going to believe me when I tell him."

"Take a picture and die. I don't want any evidence."

I turn around and face the full-length mirror for any last-minute adjustments. Between my real hair and Mac's fall, my two-color 'do should have its own zip code. The skin tone of my face is practically orange and doesn't match the rest of my body. My eyes are heavily outlined, so I look like a raccoon with two black eyes. My lips are big, red, and super shiny. And I'm wearing an adult version of a pageant dress for kids, complete with a multi-tiered (and colored) cupcake skirt, and a beaded top with organza ruffles on the sleeve.

My phone rings and Mac picks it up. "It's Mom."

I nod at her and she answers it. "Hey, Mama . . . Everything's great! No need to come up — we'll be down soon. I don't want you to see me until I'm on stage." I hold my breath. If Mac can't get Mom to stay downstairs, all of this will be ruined. "My hair looks fine. It —" Mac scowls slightly. "Mama, I told you I look good. You're making me mad, and if you keep this up I'm going to start crying and *you'll ruin everything!*" Mac's voice goes up a couple octaves and, I have to admit, I'm a little scared of her myself. "Fine." She hangs up the phone. "She's staying downstairs."

A wave of relief floods over me. Until I realize that now I have to be seen in public.

"Ready?" I say to Mackenzie.

She nods. "Thanks for doing this."

"Come on, Agent M. We've got to somehow try to make me incognito until we make it safely backstage."

We have a few close calls, but both Mackenzie and I arrive safely at the adjacent room where the contestants line up. Benny was able to hide me for most of the time, but now I'm out in the open.

And everybody's staring at me.

Holli's mom has a huge smile on her face, since it's pretty clear Mac is not competing today.

"My goodness, Lexi, I wasn't aware it's Halloween," she says with a self-satisfied smirk.

"Oh, really? Then why do you have your daughter dressed like a forty-year-old call girl?"

She glares at me and stomps away.

Mac starts to panic. "What if she gets Mom?"

"She's not going to say anything to Mom." At least I hope she isn't. I figure that all the moms are going to stay quiet if they think I'm going to do something that'll blow any chance of Mackenzie taking home a crown today. And since Mac's in jeans and a T-shirt without any makeup on, the possibilities of that happening are slim-to-none.

Cheryl, the head of the Little Miss Dallas contest, comes over to us. "You girls seem to be causing quite a scene. Miss Mackenzie, why aren't you ready?"

Mac holds on to her pageant number. "I am."

"You can't go out looking like that."

"Yes, I can. We paid the fees." Mac moves a few feet closer to the steps leading to the stage as the first person in her age division starts her beauty routine.

Cheryl looks me over. "And what's this?"

"Isn't it great?" I twirl around. "I figured when at a pageant . . ."

"We have a certain standard at Little Miss Dallas, and we will not allow you to make fools out of us."

"Believe me. I won't be making a fool out of *you.*"

I think my appearance makes it clear that the only person who's going to look idiotic today is me.

One by one, each contestant takes to the stage. We hear the emcee read the description of each girl, along with the polite applause from the audience and the catcalling from the parents.

We hear Mackenzie's name and number announced. Cheryl's glaring at both of us. I give her a smile before I step past Mackenzie and walk on stage.

There's an audible gasp from the audience, who expects to see a dolled-up seven-year-old. Instead, they see me. Or more appropriately, a clownish replica of me.

The emcee stumbles as she hesitates continuing with the script she has for Mackenzie. I take advantage of her moment of confusion to grab the microphone.

I see Mom sitting in the audience with a stunned look on her face.

"Hello, everybody," I say into the microphone. I can hear scuttling to the side of the stage. I don't have much time. "I know you weren't expecting to see me, but I had a few things that I need to say, and hope you can please extend me your courtesy for a few moments."

I feel my entire body start to shake. I've never been up on a stage before. It's a little intimidating.

"I've spent the last few years coming to these pageants, and I know that there are some of you out there who enjoy participating. I know that there are some of you who get a lot of out this. But I also know that many of you parents force this on your children. That you're making them live out some sort of fantasy for you. You shouldn't force something on your kids if they aren't happy. You should listen to your children and let them *be* kids."

A few people start shouting at me to get off the stage.

"For years, none of you would even give me the time of day. But then I started to play dress-up and got your attention. My own mother never called me beautiful until a few weeks ago. And what's sad was that I craved that kind of attention. Why? Because being pretty makes life easier? Yeah, maybe in high school, but is this really the lesson we should be teaching people? What about having substance? What about having some kind of dream that doesn't revolve around your looks, which we all know are fleeting?

"What about having fun and enjoying your childhood? Do you really think a two-year-old enjoys sitting in a makeup chair for an hour having fake eyelashes applied to her? Really? Have you asked them lately? And when did it become acceptable to drag a screaming child through a hotel lobby and force her on stage? I know that child endangerment laws are meant for more egregious acts against children, but I sometimes think those lines can be crossed at pageants."

I see something out of the corner of my eye come dangerously close to my head. I think someone threw something at me. And now there's a security officer at the side of the stage.

"But I guess I'm getting off topic, because what you decide to do with your family is your business." I move across the stage so I'm directly in front of Mom; her face is crimson red. "Hi, Mom. Will you listen to me now that I'm up on your precious stage? Do I now matter to you because I'm dressed up like a beauty queen?"

She stands up and starts to walk over.

"Mackenzie doesn't want to do pageants anymore. But you don't listen. You never listen to us unless we're saying something to please you. What kind of life is that for anybody? We're your children. When do we get to lead our own lives? When do we get to make decisions for ourselves? It's like we're prisoners in our own home because you loom over us. We have to do whatever it is that *you* want. You don't care what *we* want. What makes *us* happy."

Mom's almost to the stage when she suddenly stops. I feel a hand on my leg and look down to find Mackenzie. She takes the microphone from me.

"Stop, Mama. Lexi's telling the truth. I don't want to do this anymore. I haven't for a long time, but I didn't think you'd love me unless I did it."

I look out and see some of the mothers with their hands over their mouths or on their chests.

The heartbreaking moment is quickly interrupted as I feel my arm get yanked by a security guard. "Show's over." He pulls me offstage with a strong jerk. I stumble and fall off the small riser.

There's some applause at my embarrassing, and a little painful, fall. However, a few people come to help me up, and I can hear Benny and Cam cheering for me at the back of the room. I recover and take Mackenzie's hand.

"It's okay, we're going," I say to the security guards, who clearly weren't expecting any action at a beauty pageant.

We walk out of the room and feel every eye on us. Most of them are glaring at us with contempt. We've cast an imperfect shadow on their day. Or maybe we made a few of them think.

I feel another hand grab my arm hard.

I don't have to look over to know who it is.

"You're in so much trouble," Mom hisses.

28.

Mama's Got a Brand-new Headache

My right arm burns as Mom drags me through the hallway and into the women's restroom.

"Please, Mama!" Mackenzie cries after us. "It was my idea. Don't hurt Lexi!"

The safety pins and glue used to hold the top together start to tear away. It rips as Mom pushes me into an abandoned bathroom.

"That was some kind of stunt you pulled up there," Mom growls at me. Her face is still bright red, and a bead of sweat is making its way down her cheekbone. "How dare you embarrass your sister like that! Trying to get all the attention on her special day."

"Didn't you hear anything we said?" I try to reason with her.

"You're brainwashing your sister."

Mackenzie pulls at Mom's arm. "Mama, Lexi —"

"Enough!" she shouts at Mac.

Mac cowers at the sight of Mom. She runs over to me and buries her head into my stomach.

Mom's eyes go up and down my outfit. Recognition slowly creeps on her face.

"You better pay me back for the dresses you ruined."

I hold her gaze. "I guess we can take it from the money you owe me."

I've never seen Mom this upset before. Not even when she hit me. I'm trying to be strong for Mac, but I'm terrified of what she's going to do.

Then I see something that scares me more than the thought of her slapping me again. My mother starts to cry.

"I can't believe you would do this to me," she says softly. "You've ruined the most important thing in my life."

A wave of guilt falls over me. I know I got carried away on the stage and said things that are best reserved for family members' ears only. But I felt that this was the only way to get her to pay attention. I knew she had to take notice if we made a huge, public gesture. And while it was obvious the pageants meant so much to Mom, I didn't think they were the only thing she had in her life that mattered to her.

Shouldn't her children be the most important thing in her life?

Who am I kidding? I knew pageants were all that mattered to her. I assumed it was all about Mackenzie, but all along it was about her.

251

"Mom." I reach out my hand to her. "I'm sorry you feel that way. But Mackenzie doesn't want to do the pageants anymore, and you wouldn't listen to her. We had to do something to make you listen. To make you understand that you may enjoy the pageants, but they're tearing this family apart."

"They certainly are not." She jerks her hand away from me.

"Mom, they cost us thousands of dollars we don't have, and have made both me and Mackenzie afraid of you. What exactly have you gotten out of the pageants?"

She stays silent.

"Maybe you should take the rest of the weekend off, go somewhere. I can stay with Mackenzie and maybe you can think about what's important. Why you need these pageants. What void they fill for you. Maybe it'll help you to get some sort of perspective on how things have gone so wrong."

Mom glares at me. "How dare you give me a lecture? Like you haven't been parading around trying to impress people with your outfits and makeup. What makes you so different from me or any of the people here?"

"It doesn't," I agree. "But I've learned from my mistakes. It took me falling on my face to see what really matters to me. And it isn't looking pretty."

She folds her arms. I can't tell what she's thinking. I don't know if there's anything I can say to get through to her.

"Where do you get off talking to me like that? I'm *your mother*."

I feel my entire body start to shake. "Then start acting like it."

Mom opens up her mouth, but a woman with a Little Miss Dallas badge interrupts us. "I thought I might find you in here. The committee would like to speak to you."

Mom pushes past me without another word.

I fall down to my knees to comfort a hysterically crying Mackenzie. "It's going to be okay."

Cam comes into the room. "We saw your mom leave. Is everything okay?"

I shrug. "I don't know if things will ever really be okay between us, but the truth is out. So it's a start."

"I thought you might want this." Cam hands me my bag of regular clothes.

I quickly change out of my clothes and try to put my hair up in a ponytail, although it's so ratted I think I may just have to chop it all off. It takes eight makeup wipes to return my skin to its natural shade.

We see Benny waiting outside for us. He gives me a big hug. "You did your best. You know that, right?"

I give him a weak smile. I did what I thought would help. Mom may be mad, but Mackenzie and I have never been closer.

I take her by the hand. "Let's go home."

She smiles up at me. "You know, I was always jealous of your friends and how much people like to be around you. Someday, I hope to be as funny and clever as you."

Cam pats Mackenzie on the head. "I believe they call that a great personality."

"I hope I get one of those someday."

I squeeze her hand. "You do, Mac. You have a great personality."

"Really?"

"Really."

Cam winks at me. "So it's a good thing to have a great personality now?"

The doors of the hotel open up to a beautiful day awaiting us.

"It always has been. I was too blind to see it."

29.

The Greatest Love of All

My "little stunt" has gotten Mackenzie banned from all future Little Miss Texas–sanctioned events.

Mac and I celebrate with ice cream.

Knowing that we don't have any more pageants looming over us has, in a way, freed us. There aren't any more demands of our time or resources. Hopefully this will mean that money won't be so tight.

And above all, maybe there won't be so much tension at home anymore. Maybe we can start focusing on one another instead of a crown.

That's my hope. We haven't heard from Mom since she told us the news. She walked away without so much as a glance. Maybe she heard what I had been telling her. Maybe she's somewhere thinking about what the pageants have done to our family.

Or maybe Mac and I should go into witness protection.

Mac, Benny, and Cam are all still laughing over my outfit as I turn the car on to our street.

"Oh!" Benny slaps his forehead. "Why didn't I think of getting you on video? Hello, next Internet sensation!"

"Because you value your life . . ."

I hear Benny and Cam gasp in unison. "Guys, I'm joking —" My words get caught in my throat when I realize what they're reacting to.

There's a familiar car parked outside my house, and standing right next to it is the owner.

"Oh my God," I say under my breath.

"What's wrong?" Mackenzie looks around, trying to figure out the sudden mood change in the car.

"It's nothing."

Actually, it's Logan. Standing on our front yard.

Cam's eyes get wide. I, on the other hand, am trying to stay composed. All the drama of today made me forget about what happened last night. But now it comes flooding back to me.

Logan gives us a little wave as I park the car. He's wearing sunglasses and holding a giant bottle of water. Apparently last night hasn't completely left him.

He smiles at me, then gives me a weird look as I get out of the car. It's been weeks since Logan has seen Old Lexi in jeans and a T-shirt without a lick of makeup on. Although my hair still has enough product in it that a passing firefly could light this mess on fire.

"Hi, guys." He smiles at the group, then leans toward me. "Hey."

Oh, great, we're back to *that*?

"Ah, I'll meet you inside," I say to a concerned Benny and Cam and a clueless Mac. (Although by her smirk, I think she knows exactly what's going on.)

Mac and Benny head in the house, but Cam pauses. She comes over to me and gives me a big hug. "I'm really proud of you, for what you did today and last night," she whispers in my ear. She gives me an encouraging smile before she joins them inside.

Leaving Logan and me alone.

Memories of our last encounter fill my head.

"Hello." I sit down on the bench outside our house.

"Listen . . ." He joins me and starts shaking his right leg nervously. "Thanks for coming with me last night. I'm really sorry about getting sick and everything."

"It's okay," I say. Even though it isn't.

"I heard about what you said to Brooke. I wish I could've been conscious for that."

Yeah, me too.

"So . . ." He turns to me. "You look different."

I shrug. "This is how I looked before." I let that word hang in the air. I don't think there's a single person who doesn't realize that there was a clear *before* and *after* with me. Although now I'm somewhere in the middle.

"Oh, I thought you were — never mind," he stutters.

"It's been a rough day." I don't feel I need to give him any other explanation.

He nods slowly to himself. "Yeah, well, I was wondering when you're back to . . ." He pauses briefly, but just enough to make me wish I never put on any makeup in the first place. "Um, what I mean is that I'd like to take you out."

He hasn't even been broken up with Alyssa for two weeks and he's asking me out.

Wait a second. Logan Reeves is asking me out. Really asking me out. Not to a coffee or to the athletic dinner as *friends*. He is asking me on a date. But I think he's asking Glam Lexi, not me, just Lex.

This is everything I ever wanted. I've been dreaming, fantasizing, obsessing about this moment for years.

And now that it's here . . .

I don't really feel anything at all.

I'm realizing that Dream Logan is way better than Real Logan, which isn't fair to him. Just like Glam Me isn't fair to Normal Me.

I've built Logan up in my head as the perfect guy, but he isn't. He drinks (and apparently can't hold his liquor), he's a bad kisser, we have nothing in common now that we don't have pageants anymore, and let's face it, he's probably not over Alyssa.

I'd be the rebound girl. The girl to take his mind off of Alyssa. Who wants to be friends with him since he's *such a nice guy.*

And while I empathize with Logan more than he could probably ever realize, neither of us should be with the other for the wrong reasons.

But, in a way, this has nothing to do with Logan. It has everything to do with the person I want to be.

I know some people settle for something that they wanted (or thought they wanted), but I'm not that kind of person. I know I deserve better than that. It may have taken Benny's dares, hours of primping, family trauma, and falling on my face to come to this moment, but I finally realize that the real me is worthy of love and happiness. And it's the kind of happiness that doesn't come in the form of a boyfriend.

Especially if that guy wants to be with you for all the wrong reasons.

"Logan, what did you think about how I looked the last few weeks?"

He starts to blush. "You looked amazing."

"And before that, did you ever think of me as anything but a friend?"

He opens his mouth, then closes it. I know that it isn't fair for me to ask him. Because I already know the truth.

"Do you know that I did a lot of that stuff because of you? Because I wanted you to see me as something more than just a friend."

His face lights up. "You did?"

"Well, it wasn't my only motivation, but I did. And that isn't a good thing."

"Oh." He looks disappointed.

"All I did over the last few weeks was kill myself to get accepted by you and your friends. And to be honest, I didn't really have fun even when I was. Maybe that's because part of me knew that I didn't belong. And you know, Logan, I really like you."

"You do?" He grabs my hand.

"Yeah." I take my hand away. "But I like myself more. I'd rather be single and myself than try to fit into a mold of a person that I'm not for a guy. I know that it's not your fault that I did this, but I haven't been happy, and I think the only way for me to truly be happy is to be myself *by* myself."

"Oh, okay . . ." He takes a moment to nod to himself. "That's cool."

Logan doesn't even seem that disappointed. Probably because he knows we wouldn't make a good couple.

I give him a hug. "But I'd still like to be friends."

But unlike with Taylor, I'm not really sure how much I mean it. I think, I *hope* that Taylor and I could someday try it again. But I know I first need to concentrate on what makes me happy. And, just as important, try to heal my wounded family.

Logan and I say good-bye and I keep waiting for a small voice in my head to start screaming at me, at what I've done. But it doesn't come. Because I know I'm right.

It's very rare for fantasy and reality to line up. And in the case of Logan and me, it isn't meant to be. But I'm glad I went through what I went through. Because it made me a stronger person, and made me realize what's important.

I, Lexi Anderson, am proud to say that I do, indeed, have a *great personality*.

And it's only a matter of time before the Beautiful People will be wishing they had great personalities, too.

Good luck with that, oh Beautiful Ones.

Because we Great Girls are the rarest breed.

I Thank You, I Really, Really Thank You

I wish I could hold some sort of ceremony where I could call people up on stage and give them something, like a banner or trophy or crown, to show them how much I appreciate them. But since I don't want to scar all the amazing people in my life by making them wear flippers, gowns, fake hair, and eyelashes, this will have to suffice.

To Ultimate Grand Supreme Editor David Levithan, who was excited about this book from the moment I told him the title. Thank you for working with me to make the story stronger. I'm eternally indebted to you for your advice, friendship, music mixes, karaoke duets, and all those bus rides home.

I'm very lucky to have the Royal Queen of agents, Rosemary Stimola. Thank you for being in my corner and cheering me on (no glitter T-shirts required).

Scholastic has been an amazing publisher to work with. I'm extremely appreciative of all the work that happens behind the scenes. I don't want to think about where I would be if it weren't for the winning talents of Sheila Marie Everett (stop working so late!), Erin Black, Emily Sharpe, Tracy van Straaten (go Packers!), Bess Braswell, Stacey Lellos, Leslie Garych, Lizette Serrano, Emily Heddleson, Candace Greene, Antonio Gonzalez, Rachael Hicks, and all the reps, especially Sue Flynn, the hardest-working woman in publishing. And, of course, Elizabeth Parisi, who has spoiled me with her gorgeous covers. Sparkly tiaras for everybody!

Writing about a broken family has made me even more grateful to come from my family. Thank you to my parents and my siblings, who have stood up for and stood behind me through the years. Nobody messes with a Eulberg.

Hugs, kisses, and bedazzled sashes to my friends for their continued support of my writing career, especially Jennifer Leonard and Sarah Mlynowski. Jen has the unfortunate task of being my first reader and truly deserves a crown for that feat. And while it was incredibly intimidating for an author of Sarah's stature to read my unedited manuscript, her comments helped make this book better and her enthusiasm means the world to me (FLIPPERS!). Thanks, too, to my tour buddy, Jen Calonita, for all those fun times that cause us to lose our voices, and to

Susane Colasanti for all those chats about books, boys, Beaker, and other important things in life. And of course, Kirk Benshoff, who takes such good care of Online Elizabeth.

Huge gratitude to all the booksellers, librarians, teachers, and bloggers for your continued support. You guys ROCK and should be paid in real diamonds.

And finally, to all of those guys who told me, and my friends, that we have such great personalities, thank you for that reminder. We'll take the congeniality award any day. You were SO not worth our time.